The Man
with the
Iron-On Badge

***Other Five Star Titles
by Lee Goldberg:***

The Walk

The Man with the Iron-On Badge

Lee Goldberg

Five Star • Waterville, Maine

First Edition
First Printing: October 2005

Published in 2005 in conjunction with
Tekno Books and Ed Gorman.

Set in 11 pt. Plantin by Elena Picard.

Printed in the United States on permanent paper.

Library of Congress Cataloging-in-Publication Data

Goldberg, Lee, 1962–
    The man with the iron-on badge / by Lee Goldberg.
  —1st ed.
      p. cm.
      ISBN 1-59414-372-2 (hc : alk. paper)
      1. Private investigators—California, Southern—Fiction.
    2. California, Southern—Fiction.   3. Extortion—Fiction.
    I. Title.
    PS3557.O3577M36 2005
      813'.54—dc22   2005015987

The Man
with the
Iron-On Badge

Acknowledgements

This book would not have been possible without the enthusiasm and support of William Rabkin and Tod Goldberg and the tireless efforts of Gina Maccoby. But most of all, I have to thank my wife Valerie and my daughter Madison, without whom I'd probably be Harvey Mapes.

Chapter One

$\diamond \quad \diamond \quad \diamond$

I don't know if you've ever read John D. MacDonald's Travis McGee books before. McGee is sort of a private eye who lives in Florida on a houseboat he won in a poker game. While solving mysteries, he helps a lot of ladies in distress. The way he helps them is by fucking their brains out and letting them cook his meals, do his laundry, and scrub the deck of his boat for a few weeks. These women, McGee calls them "wounded birds," are always very grateful that he does this for them.

To me, that's a perfect world.

I wanted his life.

This is the story of what I did to get it.

My name is Harvey Mapes. I'm twenty-nine years old, six feet tall, and I'm in fair shape. I suppose I'd be better-looking if I exercised and stopped eating fast-food three times a day, but I won't, so I won't.

I'm a security guard. My job is to sit in a little, Mediterranean-style stucco shack from midnight until eight a.m. six days a week, outside the fountains and gates of Bel Vista Estates, a private community of million-dollar-plus homes in the Spanish Hills area of Camarillo, California.

The homes at Bel Vista Estates are built on a hillside above the farms of Pleasant Valley, the Ventura Freeway, and a really great outlet mall, about a quarter of the way between Los Angeles and Santa Barbara. I say that so you can appreciate the kind of drive to work I have to make each night from my one-bedroom apartment in Northridge.

There are worse jobs.

Most of the time, I just sit there looking at my black and white monitor, which is split into quarters and shows me three different views of the gate and a wide angle of an intersection up the hill inside the community. I'm supposed to watch the intersection to see if people run the stop sign, and if they do, I'm supposed to write them a "courtesy ticket" when they come through the gate.

I'd like to meet the asshole who came up with that.

It's no courtesy to give one, and the folks who live here certainly don't think it's a courtesy to take one. Most of the time, they don't even stop to get it from me; they just laugh or flip me off or ignore me altogether.

And why shouldn't they? It's not like I'm going to chase them down to the freeway or put a lien on their homes.

Enforcement really isn't my job anyway. I'm there to give the illusion of security. I don't have a gun, a badge, or even a working stapler. If there's any real trouble, which there never is, I'm supposed to call my supervisor and he'll send a car out.

The guys in the car, guys so inept and violent the police department wouldn't hire them, are the "armed response team" the company advertises. If I were a resident, I'd feel safer taking my chances with the robber, rapist, or ax murderer.

I'm just the guy in the shack. The one who either waves you through and opens the gate, or stops you to see if you've got a pass. If you do, or if I get the homeowner on the phone and he says you're okay, then I jot your name

8

and license number in my ledger, open the gate, and return to my reading.

I do a lot of reading, which is the one big perk of the job and, truthfully, the reason I took it in the first place, back when I was going to community college. Mostly I read paperback mysteries now, cheap stuff I get at used bookstores, and it's probably why I was so susceptible to his offer when it came.

I guess on some level I wanted to be like the tough, self-assured, no-problem-getting-laid guys I read about. I conveniently forgot that in a typical book, those guys usually sustain at least one concussion, get shot at several times, and see a lot of people die.

It was after midnight, but still early enough that I hadn't settled into a book yet, when Cyril Parkus drove up in his white Jaguar XJ8, the one with a forest of wood and a herd's worth of leather inside, and instead of going through the resident lane to wait for me to open the gate, he drove right up to my window.

We're supposed to stand up when they do that, almost at attention, like we're soldiers or something, so I did. The people who live at Bel Vista Estates are quick to report you for the slightest infraction, especially one that might imply you aren't acknowledging their greatness, wealth, and power.

Even just sitting in that car, Parkus exuded the kind of laid-back, relaxed charm that says to me: look how easy-going I am, it's because I'm rich and damn happy about it. He was in his mid-thirties, the kind of tanned, well-built, tennis-playing guy who subscribes to *Esquire* because he sees himself in every advertisement and it makes him feel good.

In other words, he was the complete opposite of me.

I'd see him leave for work every morning around six thirty or seven a.m., and it wasn't unusual for me to see him coming home so late. But he rarely stopped to talk to me, unless it was to leave a pass or get a package from me that his wife hadn't picked up during the previous shift. I'd only seen his wife, Lauren Parkus, once or twice, and when I did, it was late and she was in the passenger seat of his car, her face hidden in the shadows as he sped by.

"Good evening, Mr. Parkus," I said, adopting the cheerful, respectful, and totally false tone of voice I used with all the residents.

"How are you, Harvey?"

I caught him glancing at my nameplate as he spoke. Each guard slides his nameplate into a slot on the door at the start of his shift for exactly this reason. You can't expect the residents to remember, or care about, the name of the guy in the shack.

"Fine, sir," I replied. "What can I do for you?"

He smiled warmly at me, a smile as false as my cheerful respect and admiration.

"Could I ask you a couple of questions about your work, Harvey?"

"Of course, sir."

I figured there must be a complaint coming, and this was just his wind-up. In the back of my mind, I tried to guess what I could have done to piss him or his wife off, but I knew there wasn't anything.

"What are your hours?" Parkus asked.

I told him. He nodded.

"And then what do you do?" he asked.

That question had nothing to do with work, and I was tempted to tell him it was none of his fucking business, but I wanted to keep my job, and it wasn't like there was anything in my life worth keeping private. Besides, I was curious where all this was going and how I was going to get screwed in the end. At that moment, I had no way of knowing just how bad it would be or how many people would get killed along the way.

"I usually grab something to eat at Denny's, since they serve a decent dinner any time and have good prices, and then I go home."

"You go right to sleep?"

"No, sir, I like to sit by the pool if it's sunny, swim a couple of laps, maybe go to a movie or something. Then I go to bed around three in the afternoon, wake up around nine or ten, have some breakfast, and come back here for another day of work."

"So, you only work this one job and don't go to school or anything."

"That's right, sir."

Parkus nodded, satisfied. Apparently, I told him what he wanted to hear. I confirmed that I was a complete loser and that yes, his life was a lot better than mine.

"Could I meet you at Denny's in the morning and buy you dinner?" he asked. "I'd like to talk over a business proposition with you."

"Sure," I said, too stunned to say anything more.

He drove up to the gate and waited for me to open it. I hit the button, the gate rolled open, and I watched him drive up the hill, wondering what he could possibly want from me.

I kept watching him on the monitor. I couldn't do that with most residents, but Parkus happened to live on one of the corners of the intersection that I'm supposed to watch for those "courtesy tickets," so technically, I wasn't spying, I was just doing my job.

Cyril Parkus lived in a huge, Spanish-style house that had two detached garages out front and a couple of stone lions on either side of the driveway, each with one stone paw resting on a stone ball. I've never understood the point of those lion statues, or why rich people think it's classy to have them. I've thought about buying one and sticking it in front of my apartment door, just to see how my life changes, but I don't know what they're called or where you find them and I probably couldn't afford one anyway.

Once he went inside his house, the excitement was over and I was in for a long, restless night, waiting for daybreak, unaware that with the sunrise, my life would change completely.

Chapter Two

◇ ◇ ◇

At eight o'clock sharp, Victor Banos showed up for his shift. Excuse me, *Sergeant* Victor Banos. That *Sergeant* thing is real important to him, though the only real difference between him and me are two military-type stripes sewn on the shoulders of his uniform, which he earned by being the nephew of the area supervisor for the security company.

The stripes indicate that Victor gets slightly higher pay than me because he also serves as a training officer, which means he sometimes shares the shack with new recruits, showing them the complexities of writing license plates down in the log and watching the gate when you're in back on the toilet.

What Victor doesn't tell the newbies is how he takes kickbacks from painters, gardeners, plumbers, handymen, electricians, and other workers that he recommends to the residents, or that as the day-shift guy he always gets the best Christmas presents, because he's the one guard the people who live there actually know.

I really wanted Cyril Parkus to drive up in his Jag, or maybe his Mercedes or Range Rover, and pick me up for that business meeting, just to see the look of jealousy on *Sergeant* Victor's face, but I knew it wasn't going to happen.

"Anything happen last night?" asked Victor.

He asked me that every morning, and every morning I told him nothing had, even though it wasn't always true.

A year ago, in the street in front of the guard shack, I saw a coyote with a French poodle in its mouth. We stared at each other for a minute or two, then he ran off. Now the coyote shows up every few weeks to stare at me some more. I stare back. That night, just before dawn, he came back. It felt like he stared at me a lot longer this time, before loping off into the darkness.

I'm not sure if a coyote looking at me would qualify as something "happening" to Victor, who claims he once got a blowjob in broad daylight from a teenage girl who lives in the community. While she was giving it to him, her mother happened to drive up to the gate. Victor says he just smiled and waved her through, and neither mother nor daughter was ever the wiser.

I don't know if the story is true, but all of us guards wanted to believe it anyway. It gave us one more thing to fantasize about during those long shifts in that tiny shack.

So, like always, I told Victor nothing happened, and trudged down the street to where my '95 Nissan Sentra was parked, a discreet distance from the million-dollar front gate so as not to bring down the property values. They don't want my car leaking oil on the pressed-concrete cobblestones in front of the gate, but they don't mind the resident who's kept a dead DeLorean rotting in his driveway for years, the tires flat, the car caked in layers of calcified bird crap. If it was a Tercel, or a Sonata, or a Maxima, or any other car with a sticker price under fifty thousand dollars, there'd be an angry mob on his front lawn lobbing rocks, torches, and lawyers at the house.

When I got to my car, I took off my uniform shirt, stuck it on a hanger, and hung it from the plastic hook in the

14

backseat. That saved me having to wash or iron it for a couple days. I kept on the white T-shirt I wore underneath and drove down to the Ventura Freeway, took the overpass to the other side, and parked in front of the Denny's that was beside the off-ramp.

I'd been going to the Denny's since I started working at Bel Vista Estates, except for a month or two while they were remodeling the restaurant to look like a '50s diner instead of the '70s coffee shop it was before. It didn't make a lot of sense to me, since the '70s were hot again and the '50s craze was long dead, but that's Denny's for you. They'd just discovered stir-fry, too. Pretty soon they'd stumble on croissants.

I picked a booth by the window so Parkus wouldn't have any trouble spotting me. I ordered a Coke and decided to give him ten minutes before ordering, because the smell of sizzling bacon was making me drool.

I was halfway through my Coke and ten seconds away from flagging a waitress when Parkus showed up, looking like a kid sneaking into a topless bar. Not that I know much about topless bars. Well, not lately, anyway.

He smiled nervously and slid into the booth, smoothing his silk tie as if the simple act of sitting down would've wrinkled it all up. I smoothed my T-shirt, just in case sitting down had ruffled me up, too.

"Thanks for meeting me, Harvey," Parkus smiled. "I appreciate it."

I shrugged. His suit, even if he bought it at the outlet mall, was worth more than my car.

The waitress came to the table and, while I ordered a T-bone steak, fries, and another Coke, he picked up the laminated menu and made a show of looking through it. I don't think he was used to a menu with pictures on it. His discomfort already made the meeting worthwhile for me. He ended up ordering a bagel and some coffee.

As soon as the waitress was gone, he smoothed his tie again and smiled at me. I smiled back and fought the urge to smooth my T-shirt. I had no idea sitting was so hard on clothes.

"Harvey, I've got a problem and, since you're experienced in the security field, I think you're the man to help me," he said. "I need someone followed."

"Who?"

"My wife."

I knew he'd say that.

I sipped my Coke and hoped he couldn't hear my heart beating. In that instant, I'd become the hero of one of those old Gold Medal paperbacks, the ones with the lurid cover drawing of a busty girl in a bikini wrapping herself around a grimacing, rugged guy holding a gun or a martini glass.

I was now that guy.

It could happen that fast.

Then I realized that no, it couldn't. I wasn't that guy. I would never be that guy. There had to be a catch to this.

"Why me, Mr. Parkus? You could probably afford to hire a big PI firm that's got a bunch of operatives and all the high-tech stuff."

"You're right, Harvey, I could. But that would make it official, so to speak, and I want to keep this low-key."

Meaning he wanted to go cheap and pay cash out of his pocket, rather than leave a paper trail. At least that was my uneducated guess.

"Do you really want the guard out front knowing all your secrets?" I asked.

"You wouldn't know all my secrets." Parkus smiled, trying to be jovial, lighten things up. "The truth is, Harvey,

I want someone I know, someone I can talk to without creating attention. You can give me your reports as I come through the gate. No phone calls, no memos, nothing anyone can ask questions about. It's certainly not going to look strange if your car is parked outside the gate. And the great thing is, you can watch her day and night without raising any suspicion. Hell, half the time you'll just be doing your job, right out front where everybody can see you."

He'd obviously given this a lot of thought, but it still didn't make sense to me.

"Aren't you afraid she'll recognize me?"

"She's only seen you a couple of times, late at night, in the dark. I doubt she'd recognize you in the daylight, especially out of context. Besides, you're not going to get that close to her, you're too good at what you do."

Either Parkus was trying to flatter me, or he was an idiot. He had to know the extent of my surveillance experience was sitting in a chair, watching the gate open and close.

The waitress arrived with our food, which gave me a few minutes to get my thoughts together. I bought another minute or two pouring A-1 sauce on my steak and chewing on a few bites of meat. I'm glad I did, because tasting that steak cleared my head. Why was I trying to talk this guy out of hiring me? If he thought I was qualified for the job, what did I care? He was offering me the chance to play detective, which by itself was exciting, and we hadn't even started talking about the money yet.

"You think she's having an affair?" I asked.

He carefully spread some cream cheese on his bagel while he considered his answer.

"I don't think so, but something is going on. She's been acting strange, aloof, very secretive. She's evasive and can't account for her time during the day."

"I see," I said, even though I didn't. I knew more about molecular biology than I did about women, and I don't even know what molecular biology is.

It occurred to me that I didn't really know anything about this guy and that my steak was getting cold, so I said: "I'm going to need some background. What can you tell me about you and your wife?"

So, while I ate my steak and fries, Parkus told me that he worked in international distribution of movies, selling them to TV networks overseas. His office was in Studio City, a straight shot east on the Ventura Freeway. He said it took him about forty minutes in good traffic to get to work, which is where he met his wife Lauren ten years ago. She was temping as a receptionist. One day he just stepped out of the elevator and there she was. Bluebirds sang. The clouds parted. Their souls kissed. It was as if he'd known her his entire life.

He made it sound a lot more romantic and personal than that, but I was too jealous to pay attention to the exact words. You get the gist of it. They were married six months later up in Seattle, where she was from.

Lauren Parkus didn't work, and they didn't have any kids, so she spent her time on what he called the "charity and arts circuit," working on fundraisers to stop diseases, feed Ethiopians, buy Picassos for the museum, that kind of thing. And when she wasn't raising money and organizing parties, she was in charge of decorating and maintaining their home, which he told me was practically a full-time job in itself. I thought about asking him to hire me for that job when this was over, but that would have been getting ahead of myself.

Nothing, Cyril Parkus said, was more important to him than his wife and her happiness.

"Even if she's cheating on you?" I asked, and from the tight look on his face, I'd gone too far. Before he could say anything I'd regret, I kept talking. More like babbling. "I guess that's a question you won't be able to ask yourself until I find out what, if anything, is going on."

That lightened him up a little. "So you'll take the job?" Parkus asked.

"For one hundred and fifty dollars a day plus expenses."

Jim Rockford used to ask for one hundred and twenty-five dollars a day, so I adjusted up for inflation. I probably hadn't adjusted up enough, but anybody could see I wasn't James Garner, or even Buddy Ebsen, and besides, it was more than double what I got paid to guard the gate.

"What expenses?" Parkus looked amused. I tried not to look embarrassed.

"You never know, sir."

"No, I guess you don't."

Parkus reached into his pocket, pulled out a thick money clip, and peeled off five one-hundred-dollar bills onto the table.

"This should cover the first few days," he said.

It was Tuesday, so the retainer would carry me through until the weekend when, I figured, we'd review the situation and make new arrangements.

"When will you get started?" Parkus asked.

"Tomorrow, after my shift. I need to get some things sorted out today, before I jump into this."

"Of course," he replied. "Do you have a camera?"

That was one of the things I had to get sorted, but instead of admitting that, I just nodded.

"Then I guess that's it, Harvey." Parkus peeled off a twenty to cover our dinner, slid out of the booth, and stood for a moment at the edge of the table, looking down at me.

"I really hope this turns out to be nothing."

I really hoped it would take a week or so to find out.

"Me, too," I said as if I cared, which, at the time, I didn't.

He walked away and I ordered a slice of Chocolate Chunks and Chips, the most expensive pie Denny's had. I could afford it now.

Chapter Three

$\Diamond$ $\Diamond$ $\Diamond$

I live in the Caribbean.

I love saying that, and I knew that I would, which is the only reason why I chose to live in that stucco box instead of the Manor, the Palms, or the Meadows. All the buildings in that area charged the same rent for a one-bedroom with a "kitchenette," which is French for a crappy Formica counter and a strip of linoleum on the floor.

The Caribbean is built around a concrete courtyard that's got a kidney-shaped pool, a sickly palm tree, a couple plastic chaise lounges repaired with duct tape, and a pretty decent Coke machine that keeps the drinks nearly frozen, just the way I like them. The whole courtyard smells of chlorine because the manager dumps the stuff into the pool by the bucket-load. Stepping into the water is like taking an acid bath.

The tenants are evenly split between retirees, Hispanic families, Cal State Northridge students, which I was when I first moved in, and young professionals, which is what I am now. It's what losers like me like to call ourselves, so we don't feel like losers.

Carol was already at the pool when I came into the courtyard around ten. She was a young professional like me. She was my age, worked at a mortgage company, and was probably a little too chunky in the middle to be wearing a two-piece bathing suit, but I certainly wasn't going to say anything. She'd lived in the Caribbean about as long as I had and, when she was really lonely and desperate, we'd fuck sometimes. She wasn't lonely and desperate nearly as often as I'd like. It wasn't love, but we'd loaned each other money, taken care of each other when we were sick, and, like I said, fucked a few times, so you could say we were good friends.

You're probably wondering how this squares with my earlier comment that I don't know anything about women. I didn't really consider Carol a woman, for one thing. I mean, she was definitely female and she was straight, but to me a woman was more beautiful, more mysterious, more aloof than Carol. A woman was unattainable, and Carol was eager to be attained, only by a better guy than me, which I didn't blame her for. That isn't to say I understood her. I've known Carol six or seven years and she still doesn't make sense to me.

So, like I said, Carol was by the pool when I came in. I was carrying a Sav-On bag, because on the way home I'd stopped to buy myself three disposable cameras, some candy bars, two six-packs of Coke, a spiral notebook, and a couple pens. I even treated myself to the latest Spenser novel at full cover price. That's how good I felt.

I sat down on the chaise lounge next to her and set my bag on the ground between us.

"You know what's in this bag?" I asked her.

"This is not like the time you bought me some magazines with the idea I'd look in the bag and also see the big box of Trojans and think you were some kind of stud and be overwhelmed by an uncontrollable urge to hump you."

"That was years ago. When are you gonna forget about that?"

"Never," she replied. "Aren't you going to ask me why I'm sunbathing on a weekday, instead of going to work?"

"No, I want you to ask me what's in this bag."

She sighed. "Okay, what's in the bag?"

"My private eye kit." I leaned back and smiled. "Everything I need for long-term surveillance."

She leaned over and peeked in the bag. I couldn't help stealing a look at her cleavage.

"Snickers bars and a paperback." Carol leaned back on the chaise again, giving me a look. She knew where my eyes had been. "Isn't this the same as your security guard kit?"

"It's a little different," I said. "For one thing, this job pays one hundred and fifty dollars a day plus expenses."

It was an awkward segue, but I was eager to get to the big news. I took out the hundreds and waved them in front of her face. That made her sit up again.

"Where did you get that?"

"It's my retainer."

"The only retainer you know anything about is the one you wore in high school, so you can drop the bullshit. Are you doing something illegal?"

I didn't think so. And after I told Carol all the details, neither did she. But she did have questions.

"What do you know about detective work?" she asked.

"What's there to know? All I have to do is follow her," I replied. Besides, I intended to brush up on my skills that night. There was a *Mannix* marathon on TVLand I was going to watch, and I'd have the new Spenser book to refer to during the lulls in my surveillance.

"So you're going to keep working your midnight-to-eight

shift and follow her during the day."

"That's right."

"If you're supposed to watch her all day, when are you going to sleep?"

"At one hundred and fifty dollars a day plus expenses, who needs sleep?"

"This should be interesting."

"Which is why I'm doing it. When was the last time my life was interesting?"

Carol smiled. "You have a point."

She wasn't lonely or desperate or in the mood to help me celebrate in the lusty way I thought we should, so I went to my apartment to prepare for my new job.

My apartment is a second-floor unit with a "lanai," which is Hawaiian for a tiny little deck you can barely fit a lawn chair on, and has a spectacular view of our dumpster, which is usually left wide open. So I use the "lanai" to store stuff, like a bike I haven't used in four years, a hibachi grill, and that lawn chair I mentioned.

My place is decorated in a casual style I like to call Thrift Shop Chic. Most of my furniture comes from garage sales and hand-me-down stores, with the exception of my bed, which is just a mattress and box spring on a wrought-iron frame. I practically live on this big, black, leather couch I bought at the Salvation Army for a hundred bucks that'd been softened up and creased all over by years of pounding by heavy butts long before I got it.

I've also got a bunch of those white particle-board book-cases, the kind you put together with those little, L-shaped, screw-in-tool thingies that come in the box. Most of the shelves are sagging under the weight of books, videos, and stereo components, but it doesn't bother me as long as the bookcases don't collapse.

I took a frosty can of Coke from the fridge, a bag of chips from the cupboard, and settled on my couch, put my feet up on the coffee table, and turned on the TV set.

For the next six hours, I watched *Mannix* reruns on TVLand and here's what I learned.

Getting shot in the arm, which happened to Joe at least three times that afternoon, is really no more painful or debilitating than pulling a muscle. A few days with your arm in a sling and you're fine. You can also relieve the pain of a concussion by just rubbing the back of your neck and shaking your head. However, you can probably avoid a concussion altogether, if before you walk through a door you peek around the corner first; that way, no one can surprise you with a karate-chop to the back of your neck.

Picking a mobster's henchmen out of a crowd isn't really too hard. They are usually the grimacing, muscle-bound guys who look very uncomfortable in their turtleneck sweaters and blazers. They will also be staring at you menacingly, which is a good tip-off about their intent.

I also learned some important pointers about following people. If you're a private eye, to follow someone driving, you just have to stay one car behind your target; and to tail him walking on the street, stroll casually ten yards back and pretend to window-shop and you'll never be noticed. However, if you're a private eye and someone is following one car behind you, you will spot him immediately; and if anyone is shadowing you while you're walking on the street, you can usually see him by checking out your reflection in a store window.

It's a good idea for a private eye to drive a sports car of some kind, especially if you want to get away from someone by driving around corners real fast, your tires screeching.

Intelligent, well-educated criminals drive Cadillacs or Lincolns, psycho killers and thugs drive Chevys or pickup trucks, while just about every law enforcement officer thinks he will be inconspicuous in a stripped-down, American-made sedan with a huge radio antenna on the trunk.

If you have a female client, no matter what she says, deep down she wants to fuck you. The same goes for any other woman you meet, especially waitresses, secretaries, nurses, and strippers. Apparently, nothing is sexier to a woman than a private eye doing his job. That bit of information was especially nice to know.

Hey, I'm not some kind of cartoon character. I knew *Mannix* wasn't the real world, that if, say, someone shot me in the arm, I'd probably piss myself and start weeping in agony, then spend the next few weeks zoned out on painkillers I couldn't afford. But I figured any knowledge was better than nothing at all, and that I couldn't help but pick up a few useful pointers from watching a private eye, even a fictional one, at work.

Maybe they used real private eyes as technical advisors on the show. Who knows?

By three p.m. I thought I was ready for bed, but it turned out I was too keyed up to sleep, even though all I'd done was watch TV and eat Cheetos all day. So I put my favorite whack-off tape, *The Wild Side*, into the VCR and went back to the couch.

The tape was already cued up to the scene where Anne Heche and Joan Chen have simulated, lesbo sex, but in light of Anne's later frolicking with Ellen DeGeneres, I like to think her lust was real. Though you got to wonder if Anne had made it with Joan Chen, why she would want to rub herself against Ellen DeGeneres. Put Joan and Ellen

26

side-by-side naked and, whether you're a man or a woman, the choice is obvious.

Anyway, I watched the tape, jerked off, and thirty seconds later, I was ready for bed again. This time, I had no trouble falling asleep.

I dreamed I was Joe Mannix, wearing the checked blazer and all, tooling around in a Dodge Charger convertible with Joan Chen in the backseat, her shirt open to her crotch.

Even asleep, I knew it was just a dream, but I also thought that it could actually happen.

Chapter Four

◇ ◇ ◇

The drive from Northridge to Camarillo takes you out the northwestern end of the San Fernando Valley, past the wealthy, four-car garage suburbs of Calabasas, Agoura, Thousand Oaks, and Westlake Village, and down the Conejo Pass into Pleasant Valley.

Around Camarillo, the number of Mercedes, Volvos, BMWs, and Range Rovers thins out and you see a lot of farm workers crammed into shitcans like mine. The area between Camarillo and Santa Barbara is filled with farms, and it takes a lot of low-paid, mostly Hispanic workers to do all the planting and picking.

The area is considered far enough from real places like LA and Santa Barbara that there are two big outlet malls for travelers who find themselves caught in the middle of the two-hour journey between the two cities with no place to shop.

Above all of this, looking down on everything like the imperious Greek gods in those old Hercules movies, are the people who live in the gated communities on the graded peaks of Spanish Hills.

On the off-chance that those farm workers ever rise up in violent revolt and storm the hills, they've got to get past the guard in the shack first.

I like to think that the terrifying prospect of rousing me from reading a paperback is what keeps them in line.

The night before my first day as a detective went fast. The only memorable moment was the flash of breast I saw while staring at the scrambled picture of the cable porn channel on TV. That was another perk of the job I forgot to mention.

I practically ran out of the shack when Victor showed up in the morning. I didn't want to get caught by surprise, just in case Lauren Parkus decided to meet her lover promptly at eight a.m.

I hustled down the street to my car, which was parked beside the grassy embankment, and changed into a polo shirt and sunglasses as a disguise. As soon as I was in the car, I stripped off my uniform pants and put on jeans. Actually, that was a lot harder than it sounds, and I was really afraid Lauren Parkus would pick that moment, while my feet were up against the dashboard and I was struggling with my pants, to leave for her erotic romp.

But she didn't.

In fact, she was taking so long to get going that I was getting mightily pissed. I was eager to begin detecting, and she was sapping my enthusiasm by not doing her part.

I sat there for two hours, my hands on the steering wheel, staring at the gate, playing out various surveillance scenarios in my mind, and I got so into it that when she finally drove out in her Range Rover, I thought it was an illusion.

I resisted the temptation to stomp on the gas pedal and instead showed my calm professionalism by easing into traffic, not that there was any. I was the only other car on the road, so I stayed way back behind her until we got down into the sprawl of shopping centers and gas stations.

The traffic was pretty heavy down there, so I hesitantly let two cars slip between us. It was a good thing she was driving such a high car, or I would have had a hard time following her.

She turned into the Encino Grande Shopping Center and parked right in front of a place called The Seattle Coffee Bean. I parked in one of the aisles so I could watch her inconspicuously. Lauren went inside and ordered something. I deduced it was coffee.

My hand was shaking as I made a notation in a notepad of her activities. All she did was buy a cup of coffee and my heart already was pounding with excitement. If this kept up, I figured I'd have a stroke when her stud finally appeared.

She sat down at a table outside and took her time sipping her coffee. It gave me a chance to really look at her for the first time.

Lauren Parkus was in her early thirties, with long, black hair and the same lean physique and tennis tan as her husband, which made sense to me. They probably worked on it together, unless she was bonking her tennis pro. I figured I'd soon find out which it was.

Her face had a sculpted beauty, as if God was concentrating very hard while he was working on her slender nose, her sharp cheekbones, the gentle curve of her chin, and her long, graceful neck.

She was clearly deep in thought over something, giving her a pensive expression that did nothing to dull the startling intensity of her eyes, which I could feel from twenty yards away.

She wore a large, loose-fitting blouse that was casually unbuttoned down to the swell of her perfect breasts. And I mean *perfect,* the kind of breasts you only see on women on movie posters, book covers, and comic books.

I picked up one of the disposable cameras and snapped a picture. It wasn't for Cyril Parkus. It was for me.

Lauren was beautiful.

It took her a half an hour to finish her coffee; then she drove off across the parking lot. I was right behind her, I mean literally, as she stopped for traffic at the exit. She glanced into the rearview mirror and I ducked down, as if searching for a station on the radio.

When I looked back up, praying that she hadn't seen my face, Lauren had already shot into traffic on Las Posas. I tried to follow, but nobody would let me in. It was bumper-to-bumper and the space between the cars and the sidewalk was too narrow for me to fit into. I watched in desperation as she sped through the intersection and on towards the freeway onramp.

If I didn't get through the intersection before it turned red, she'd hit the freeway and I'd never catch up to her.

I swore, turned the wheel, and hit the gas, speeding with half my car on the road, the other half on the sidewalk, the underbelly of my Sentra scraping the curb and spraying sparks as I went. But Lauren didn't see any of that; her Range Rover had already disappeared down the embankment to the freeway.

I made it through the intersection as the light turned yellow, and raced onto the freeway in time to see Lauren's Range Rover about five cars ahead of me.

I weaved through cars until I'd cut the number of cars between us down to two, then I relaxed, settling back into my vinyl seat, noticing for the first time that my entire body was drenched with sweat.

I'd almost lost her and yet, the truth is, I loved every desperate moment.

★ ★ ★ ★ ★

I spent the next forty-five minutes on the freeway into Santa Barbara torturing myself, wondering if I'd screwed up and she'd done all that on purpose to lose me.

But if Lauren had, she wasn't making it too hard for me to keep up with her.

Then a Highway Patrol car roared up behind me, tailgating me for a while and giving me something new to worry about. I convinced myself he could tell I was stalking this beautiful woman and he was just waiting for back-up before arresting me. But after a mile or two, he got off the freeway and let me go back to torturing myself over previous events.

The further north we got, the foggier and cooler it got. It's what my mother used to call "beach weather." She liked it misty and gray like that. I don't know why. I suppose it's one of the things I might have asked her, if she hadn't walked out the door one morning when I was fourteen and decided not to come back.

That's around the time I started reading mysteries. I began with Encyclopedia Brown, which I liked for the tough puzzles and the simmering erotic tension. I kept waiting for him to cop a feel from Sally, the prettiest girl in the fifth grade and the only kid in school who could kick the shit out of that bully Bugs Meany, but if it ever happened, I missed it.

I went from Encyclopedia to the Hardy Boys, and then at a garage sale I stumbled onto a pile of ratty, old paperbacks by Richard Prather. He wrote about Shell Scott, a detective who, like me, had a twenty-four-hour-a-day hard-on and looked like a freak. Shell was six feet tall with white hair and white eyebrows. I was gawky and covered with zits. He got laid all the time by women he called tomatoes. I masturbated a lot.

When I wasn't reading or jerking off, I watched PI shows on TV. We had a great UHF station that showed all the old stuff, everything from *77 Sunset Strip* to *Cannon*. The PIs on The Strip, they were cool cats, even though one of the detectives was played by an actor named Efrem Zimbalist, Jr. If a guy with a name like Efrem could fool people into thinking he was cool, maybe Harvey Mapes wasn't such a geek name after all. Private Eye Frank Cannon was an ugly fat-ass, but I admired how he the got the job done anyway. I thought it'd be great if in one episode he overpowered a hitman by sitting on him, but I don't think he ever did.

Lauren took the first off-ramp into Santa Barbara, where Kinsey Milhone lives, though she calls it Santa Teresa, which doesn't fool anybody. I followed Lauren as she drove along the broad beach and I wondered which of the hotels she'd end up at. She had her choice of meticulously maintained, retro-style motels or one of the lush, expansive resorts. They were all pricey and only a few stories tall to maintain Santa Barbara's friendly village ambience and ensure unobscured views of the offshore oil rigs.

I figured she'd choose a motel, because even at three hundred fifty bucks a night, there was still a certain dirty charm to a room you could drive up to.

But she surprised me by driving past the pier, and the turn into the downtown shopping district, and heading into the beach parking lot instead. She paid her two bucks and found a spot. I did the same, noting the expense, the time, and the location in my notebook and admiring my own professionalism.

Lauren got out of her car, took off her shoes, and walked out on to the sand. I stayed where I was and just watched her.

She walked down to the shore and strolled with her bare

feet in the surf. I waited expectantly for the illicit rendez-vous and two hours later, my bladder bursting, it still hadn't happened.

Lauren just sat on the sand, staring at the waves. For me, looking at all that churning surf only made my predicament worse.

I kept glancing at the restrooms, trying to gauge how long it would take me to run inside, piss, and come back out, and if she could disappear in that time. I was never good at math or geometry.

I decided to take a chance.

I bolted out of the car and ran into the restroom, which was thick with flies and the fetid stench of urine. I hurried up to a urinal and pissed. It seemed to take forever. And while I was doing it, I became aware of a homeless man sitting on the floor in a corner, staring at me furiously, like I'd broken into his house and started pissing on his rug.

As I zipped up my fly, I smiled at him and actually said I was sorry. I ran out, took a deep breath of fresh air, and looked at the beach.

She was gone.

I couldn't believe it. I'd only been away a few seconds and she'd disappeared. I looked for her car. It was still there, so she couldn't have gone far.

Unless she got into her lover's car.

I told myself there wasn't time for that to happen. She'd been down by the water, she couldn't have gotten back to the parking lot that quickly.

I ran out towards the water, looking everywhere for her as I went.

And that's when I almost stepped on her.

She was right where she was supposed to be, only now she was lying down, which is how I'd missed her. I quickly spun around, turning my back to her, and hoped for the second time that day that she hadn't noticed me.

I walked quickly back to my car, got inside, and gave some thought to how to avoid pissing on duty in the future.

I passed the time reading the Spenser book and noticed he never had bladder issues on the job, which I now knew from experience wasn't very realistic. I was thinking about writing a letter on the subject to the author when Lauren got up off the sand and trudged back towards her car.

I made a notation of the time and started my car up in anticipation.

As Lauren got closer, I could see the sadness on her face. Perhaps it was longing for the lover who never showed up. I briefly considered volunteering to take his place, but ethically, it just wasn't the right thing to do. I also lacked the courage, the looks, and the charm to pull it off. But there was a light, cool breeze buffeting her blouse, making her nipples big and hard, so I couldn't help at least fantasizing about the possibility.

I took another picture. This one was also for me.

She got in her car, backed out slowly, and drove off. I took it easy and let a couple cars pass before leaving the parking lot and following her down the street the way we came.

It was going just fine until we were nearly at the freeway. She went through the intersection and the light turned yellow on the car that was between us.

There was only one way to stay with her.

I ran the red light.

The only thing I really remember about the accident was the sound of the impact when the van clipped me.

I don't know what it felt like when the car rolled over all

those times, or what I was thinking when I unbuckled my seat belt, crawled out of my upside-down Sentra, and vomited on the pavement.

What is real clear to me was the terror on the face of the van's Mexican driver as he slowed to look at me, and then the sound of his tires squealing as he sped off, dragging his front grill along the pavement.

Chapter Five

$\diamondsuit$ $\diamondsuit$ $\diamondsuit$

In a strange way, it was my lucky day.

The driver of the van that hit me must have been an il-legal alien or a wanted criminal or something, because he didn't stick around to accuse me of running the red light and causing the accident.

That wasn't the only break I got.

The witnesses were totally unreliable. Because the driver of the van fled, in their minds that made him the bad guy, even though they must have seen me run the red light. They resolved the conflict between what they saw and what really happened by simply changing what they saw.

I helped things along by looking as pitiful and pained as I possibly could, hoping to appeal to their compassion and gullibility.

It worked.

To the police, I was the poor victim of a hit-and-run driver and he became the asshole who hit me. Obviously, I didn't say anything that would change their minds, but now I know what eyewitness testimony is really worth.

I also made sure to describe the Hispanic driver as black, and say, with absolute certainty, that his Chevy van was a Ford. The last thing I wanted the police to do was find the guy, and the witnesses helped me again. One witness described the driver as Asian, another saw a white woman, and no one knew what kind of van it was.

The paramedics insisted that I go to the hospital, but I didn't want to make a bad day worse by adding a medical deductible to my problems. Besides, all I had were a few cuts and bruises, which they'd already doctored up just fine. So I swallowed four Advils, thanked them, and walked away to inspect what was left of my Sentra.

There was no question that my car was totaled. I was insured, but I had a thousand-dollar deductible to keep my rates down. I doubted my car was worth much more than two grand, and with only seven hundred eighty-eight dollars in the bank, I saw financial disaster in my future.

I borrowed a cop's cell phone and called my insurance agent, and discovered my luck was still holding. The deductible didn't apply in this situation. The insurance company had a deal with a body shop in Santa Barbara; all I'd have to do is have my car towed there and they'd take care of everything, even give me a free rental until they could cut me a check for the negligible market value of my heap.

I figured if I kept working for the next week or so at both jobs, I could still come out of this ahead financially and with a car no worse than what I had before.

So, while I waited for the tow truck, I salvaged my uniform, cameras, and notebook from the car and tried to figure out how I was going to hide this huge fuck-up from Cyril Parkus.

I glanced at my watch. It was five twenty-five.

Lauren Parkus could be anywhere. Fucking her lover or robbing banks or hopping a jet to Rio, for all I knew.

Cyril Parkus was going to want a complete account of his wife's activities, and if I made something up, I stood a good chance of being caught.

What would happen, for example, if I reported that she went to the movies at three, but when Cyril Parkus got home he discovered his wife had bought a couple stone lions for their back door? Her shopping trip wouldn't be in my report and I'd be outed as a moron.

The last time I'd seen Lauren was two hours ago, getting onto the southbound Ventura Freeway. If I was very, very, very lucky, she went straight home, but I didn't hold out much hope.

It was after eight by the time I got out of Santa Barbara in my rented Kia Sephia, Korea's idea of an automotive practical joke. I was certain if I hit a speed bump too fast, I would be killed instantly.

Even so, I drove the car as fast as it would go, managing to nudge the speedometer all the way up to fifty-six miles per hour without the engine bursting into flames and covering the freeway with bits of charred hamster.

All in all, my first day doing detective work wasn't quite what I'd hoped it would be. There was no glamour. There was no action. And the only nipples I saw were from a distance. It was a complete disaster. Even so, I was exhilarated in a way I hadn't been since—well, since ever.

I knew I wasn't going to have time to go home before starting my shift, so I stopped at Target and reluctantly parted with fifty bucks. I bought a fresh shirt and pants, a battery-operated alarm clock, a bunch of snack food, and some personal hygiene stuff.

I stopped at a Chevron station and cleaned myself in the restroom. I shaved, brushed my teeth, and washed my hair in the corroded sink. I slathered Arrid Extra Dry Ultra Fresh Gel under my arms, shook the broken glass off my uniform, and put it on, hoping no one would notice in the dark just how wrinkled and dirty it was.

Exuding ultra-freshness, I got back in my car and drove to Spanish Hills, parking down the block from Bel Vista Estates. I set the alarm clock for eleven fifty, put it on the dash, and closed my eyes.

The alarm rang on time. I swiped it off the dash and stuck it in the glove box, which I discovered was roomier than the trunk. I made a mental note to myself to scratch the Kia Sephia off my list of possible new cars.

Every part of my body ached from the accident and within seconds of waking up, my stomach started cramping with anxiety. I still had no idea what I was going to tell Cyril Parkus. I didn't want him to find out I was incompetent, at least not until I got more of his money, which I needed more now than ever.

I got out of the car, told myself I was as ultra-fresh as I smelled, and walked up to the shack to relieve Clay Denbo, sort of a younger version of me, only black and two hundred pounds heavier. I weigh one ninety, so you get the picture.

Clay worked part-time while going to community college in Moorpark, the way I did, only I went to Cal State Northridge, which is a better school.

He was thinking of either becoming a radio psychologist or a parking concepts engineer. Redesigning the layout of parking lots to add more spaces was kind of his hobby. He had a whole sketchpad of ideas he carried around with him and was always asking me to keep my eyes open for problem parking areas he could visit.

Clay was packing up his textbooks and sketchpad as I walked up. One of the books was called *The History of Vehicle Parking in the Urban Landscape*, a real grabber. He took one look at me and his mouth kind of hung open.

"Jesus Christ, Harvey, what happened to you?" he asked.

"A woman," I replied. It wasn't exactly a lie, but the implication was certainly dishonest.

Clay broke out in a big grin, and I realized he'd make a terrific black Santa Claus and, with the political correctness and diversity thing being trendy at the time, I thought it might even be a money-making idea for him. But I kept the idea to myself, not sure if it'd be taken as some kind of racist jab. You can't be too sure these days.

"Hot damn," Clay said. "Looks like she crawled all over you."

"She really likes a man in uniform." I smiled.

"Think she'd go for a lot more man in a lot more uniform?"

"I hope not."

Clay gave me a jolly slap on the back as he stepped out of the shack. "See you tomorrow, stud."

As soon as he was gone, the first thing I did was rewind the tapes from the gate's surveillance cameras until I came across Lauren Parkus returning home.

I froze the tape on her Range Rover going through the gate. According to the time code, she drove in at four seventeen, not even an hour after I last saw her.

That meant she drove straight home. She couldn't have stopped anywhere between Santa Barbara and the gate in that amount of time.

I fell into the chair and nearly cried with relief.

I had a second chance.

Cyril Parkus drove out of the community and up to the shack around seven thirty in the morning.

"So?" he asked.

I gave him my handwritten report. "She had coffee, took a walk on the beach, and came home."

Parkus didn't look up from the piece of notebook paper, as if staring at it real hard would reveal new details even I had missed.

"She didn't see anybody all day?" he asked.

"Not unless you count the guy who served her coffee."

"I see you noted the seven dollars you paid for parking," he said. "That would be one of the expenses you were talking about."

"Yes, sir."

"The one hundred and fifty dollars a day doesn't cover parking?"

I couldn't tell if he was playing with me, or just being cheap. He didn't wait for me to answer, he just handed the paper back to me.

"Thanks, Harvey," he said. "Keep up the good work."

And with that, Cyril Parkus drove off, the smell of leather upholstery lingering in his wake.

He didn't even say anything about how lousy I looked. Maybe I really was ultra-fresh. Or maybe he just didn't give a damn.

Sergeant Victor Banos showed up a few minutes later, and he made up for Parkus' oversight regarding my appearance. I won't share all the snide remarks he made, they really aren't pertinent to the story. Needless to say, I got out of there as fast as I could, returned to my Sephia, and changed into my new clothes.

I'd just got my pants on when Lauren Parkus drove out of the gate. She was getting a very early start. I turned the key in the ignition, hit the gas pedal in my stocking feet, and followed after her.

Lauren didn't make it difficult for me this time. She

went right down to the freeway and headed south. We hit the tail end of rush hour traffic, so keeping up with her was easy, though my Sephia struggled mightily going up the Conejo Pass between Camarillo and Newbury Park. The car was such a little shitcan, I was afraid if a bug slammed into the windshield the car would be totaled.

She took me across the San Fernando Valley to Studio City, where she got off at Coldwater Canyon and headed south towards the Hollywood Hills.

I stayed one car behind her on Coldwater and tailgated the guy in front of me. I was afraid of another intersection mishap like the day before. If this guy raced into the intersection on a yellow, I was going too, hanging right onto his bumper. We crossed Ventura Boulevard without incident, but the guy in front of me got spooked and made a sharp, last-minute right turn onto a side street.

I bet the idiot thought I was following him.

She led me up Coldwater and I relaxed a bit because I had a general idea where we were headed. Coldwater weaves through the Hollywood Hills and is basically used as a shortcut between the Valley and Beverly Hills.

So I settled back and enjoyed the drive. We passed one big mansion after another. They aren't so much homes as they are billboards. The only reason anybody that wealthy would want to live on a busy, narrow street like that is to show everybody how much money he has.

So for the opportunity to brag, these rich-ass people get to breathe exhaust fumes and listen to traffic going by all day.

In other words, they're paying millions to experience what it's like living in a cardboard box beside a freeway.

Just because the rich have money, it doesn't mean they've got brains.

43

I followed Lauren Parkus across Sunset, where Coldwater becomes Beverly Boulevard and widens quite a bit. The houses are every bit as expensive and just as showy. You'll also find a lot more of those mysterious stone lions.

She crossed Santa Monica Boulevard and entered the fancy shopping district known in all the tourist guides as the Golden Triangle, which sounds like a sleazy euphemism for a woman's crotch. Based on the name, you'd expect to find topless bars and nudie shows instead of Ralph Lauren, Gucci, and Tiffany's. Then again, the most famous street in the area is Rodeo Drive, but you won't find anything that even remotely has to do with rodeos, cattle, or cowboys. So right away you know nothing in Beverly Hills is what it says it is, or appears to be.

Lauren drove into one of the city-owned, valet parking lots. I pulled in a couple of cars behind her, then ducked down to put on my shoes as she walked past me. When I gave my keys to the valet, he looked like I dropped a turd in his hand.

I walked about a half-block behind Lauren and carried my Kodak disposable camera out in the open, figuring that way I'd look like a tourist and wouldn't raise any suspicions if people saw me taking pictures. Not that anyone was going to notice me with so many boob jobs walking by.

These tomatoes were mostly plastic fruit. The women here seemed to be walking around for the sole purpose of modeling their new hooters. I wondered how many of them would sleep with me if I had white hair and white eyebrows. They'd probably just run screaming. I gladly took in the show, but was careful not to let my attention stray too long.

Besides, it wasn't like watching Lauren was painful on the eyes. She was wearing trim, black linen pants and a sleeveless, white top, and I found the aggressive, don't-give-me-shit way she was walking down the street incredibly sexy. Gone was any of the pensiveness she seemed to have yesterday. Today she seemed pissed off and in a hurry.

I liked it.

Remember how earlier I was talking about what a woman was? Lauren Parkus was a woman. No doubt about it.

She marched up to the door of Beverly Hills Collateral Lenders and hesitated. Just for a moment. Like she'd changed her mind. She made a quarter-turn in my direction, and that's when I snapped a picture.

I only saw her face for an instant, but I thought I saw fear, anger, and sadness all mixed together. I felt the surprising urge to hold her. Not for sex, either, which was the most surprising part about it. In the time it took for the shutter to click, whatever doubts Lauren had disappeared and she went inside.

I stood where I was and took a good look at Beverly Hills Collateral Lenders. There were no windows, just a sign in elegant script and a door squeezed between a clothing store and an overpriced muffin place. Although I couldn't see inside, I could guess what she was doing and it made me angry.

I bought a five-dollar cranberry muffin and a two-dollar cup of coffee, sat down at a table out front, and waited to see what happened next.

Chapter Six

◇　◇　◇

"Collateral Lender" is just a fancy way of saying "Pawn Shop."

I know a few things about pawn shops. I've never been inside one myself, but my father was a regular customer and that's how I acquired my knowledge and a healthy hatred of the places.

My father, Kingston "King" Mapes, was a gambler. I tell that to most people, and they imagine some suave guy in a tuxedo, striding into a ritzy casino. Or they think of that Kenny Rogers song.

He was nothing like either one, and I suspect that's true of most people who play cards and call themselves gamblers like it's something to be proud of.

I suppose I should have been angry about paying seven dollars for a muffin and a cup of coffee, instead of things that happened in the past. I was stuck with the past, I couldn't do anything about that, but I certainly wasn't going to patronize that muffin place again. You could get two big breakfasts at Denny's for the same price.

Like I said, rich people sometimes aren't very bright when it comes to spending what they've earned. It's a good thing I was on an expense account.

I glared some more at the Beverly Hills Collateral

Lenders sign and wondered what Lauren's problem was. Maybe her lover needed some quick cash. Maybe it wasn't a lover, maybe it was drugs. Or maybe she was a gambler like my dad. If she was, pretty soon Cyril's house would be stripped clean of anything of value. When I was a kid, my dad once stole my watch and clock radio while I was sleeping. I woke up one morning and they were gone. That's why, to this day, I sleep with my watch on.

After staring at the building for a while, it occurred to me I hadn't seen her go in carrying anything but her purse. Maybe she wasn't there to hock stuff, maybe she was there to buy things. Could be I'd totally misjudged her. Could be she was actually being a crafty shopper. The goods here had to be better than the stuff at your average pawn shop.

That thought made me feel a lot better, until she walked out ten minutes later, empty-handed. Lauren stood outside the door for a minute, looking kind of dazed. I took a couple pictures. I didn't want to hug her any more. I wanted to slap her. But I didn't have to call Dr. Laura to know I really wanted to slap my father.

I could slap him any time I wanted. He's in his sixties now, living in Palm Springs, near the Indian casinos. I actually visit him sometimes, in his crummy little bachelor unit at the Tropic Palms apartments. He likes to call me Prince.

I've never slapped him, but my sister Becky once slapped me when she found out I went down there. I don't think she was slapping me, really, but maybe I'm over-analyzing things. People who know my father and me, and there aren't many, say I look just like him.

But none of this has anything to do with Lauren Parkus, or the terrible things that happened later, and that's what I'm supposed to be talking about.

Lauren walked slowly back to her car. Whatever was

pushing her along before was gone. I think she didn't want to go back. I took more pictures. It was really just an excuse to look at her some more, like I'd be able to understand her better through the lens than with the naked eye. Which was stupid. It was a disposable camera, not a fucking microscope.

She paid the valet, got in her car, and drove off. I did the same.

Lauren Parkus got back to Bel Vista Estates before lunchtime. I parked in my usual spot alongside the embankment, where I was out of sight of the guard shack but could still see if anyone left or entered the community.

After about two hours, I slid over to the passenger seat, opened the door a crack, and pissed onto the street from a sitting position. I didn't want some homeowner driving by and seeing me taking a leak; that would get me fired for sure. So there I was, in my Sephia, sitting there pissing out the door, which isn't as easy as you might think if you don't want to wet yourself or the car.

Being in that vulnerable position, I was certain that's when Lauren would decide to leave again, but she didn't. I didn't know it then, but I was in for a long, boring afternoon.

I listened to Dr. Laura, reread my two-line report a few times, ate a box of Ritz crackers, a bag of beef jerky, and a package of Ding Dongs, and tried hard not to fall asleep.

I'd been up over twelve hours already and hadn't had much sleep the day before, which was when I really could have used it, after that accident and all.

At five o'clock, I decided to leave.

Now that might not sound very professional to you, but here was my thinking: Her husband usually came home between six and eight, and occasionally later, so she wasn't likely to run off during that period. The only risk was that she would sneak out in the hour between five and six.

But I needed to get my film developed, and most of those one-hour photo places closed by six or seven. I also needed to get my uniform cleaned and pressed and go home for a nap, a shower, and fresh clothes.

And I was exhausted and felt like shit.

All things considered, I was willing to take the risk.

Maybe Spenser wouldn't do it, but he has Hawk to help him out. It's easy to be a complete professional when you've got some big, black muscle to back you up with the unpleasant and tedious aspects of the job.

I dropped off my film at the Thrifty near my house, and my uniform at the dry cleaner next door, then went into Ralph's and browsed through the magazines while I waited for both items to be ready.

The photos were done first, so I took them with me over to Fat Burger for a quick dinner. I was careful not to dribble anything on the pictures as I looked through them.

The first thing that struck we was how her eyes blazed, even in a photograph. The moment was frozen but her eyes were alive.

I felt the irrational fear that she might actually be able to see me and then I found, weirdly, that I wished she could.

I attributed the feelings to hunger and lack of sleep, because otherwise they didn't make any sense.

I studied the pictures, first because I thought she was beautiful, and I was surprised that a cheapo camera like the Kodak disposable managed to capture the darkness of her hard nipples under her blouse. But then I studied the pictures for another reason. Something had changed about her over the two days, and I couldn't figure out what it was.

Her clothes were different, of course, and the expressions on her face covered a lot of emotional range, but otherwise I couldn't tell what had changed. But I knew something had. I could feel it.

I finished my burger, and went back to Thrifty and bought a magnifying glass before picking up my uniform next door.

When I got back to my car, I hung my uniform up in the backseat, got inside, and looked at the pictures again, this time with the magnifying glass. I had no idea what I was looking for, but it seemed like the professional thing to do. I figured there must be a reason why the magnifying glass is the universal logo for private eyes.

I looked her over real good. She may have been the most beautiful woman with the most perfect body I'd ever seen. And then there were those eyes, like the tractor beams Captain Kirk was always using to capture objects in space. Once you were locked in a tractor beam, good luck escaping without a fight.

I moved the magnifying glass slowly down her slender neck, almost like a caress, to professionally scrutinize the rest of her perfect body.

And then I noticed it, and I went back quickly over all the pictures to make sure.

I sat back and smiled at myself in the rearview mirror. I had just accomplished my first piece of true detecting based on instinct, investigation, and deduction.

In my mind, at that moment, I became a detective.

I was drying off from my shower and getting ready for bed around seven p.m. when there was a knock at my door.

I could tell from the knock it was Carol, so I just yelled for her to come in.

It's not that we had a secret knock or anything like that, she just knocks a certain way. Maybe there's a rhythm to it or something.

I put on my terrycloth robe and walked into the living room, which means I also walked into the kitchen, den, and library at the same time.

"How's it going, Magnum?" Carol smiled. She was still in her Anne Klein suit, the one she bought on sale and was so proud of, so I knew she'd just come from work without even stopping by her apartment first.

Actually, I didn't know she did that. I deduced it. I wondered if maybe I'd been a detective longer than I'd thought.

"You weren't home last night," she said. "Did you get lucky?"

"I was on the case."

"Uh-huh." She went to the fridge and helped herself to a Coke. "What happened to your car?"

"What do you mean?" I asked quickly. For a minute, I was afraid that somehow she'd found out about the accident.

"There's a new car parked in your spot." She sat down on the couch and put her feet up on the coffee table.

"It's just something I rented so I wouldn't be noticed," I said, trying to sound casual. "But I am thinking, when this is over, of getting rid of my junker."

I added that last part to cover the inevitable purchase of a new ride.

"What happened to your forehead?" she asked.

I reached up and felt a little lump on my brow, probably a bruise from the accident.

"Nothing. It's just what happens when I think too hard,"

I said. I really was in a hurry to get to the parts of my story that would impress her, not the stuff that made me look like an oaf. "So, do you want to hear about the case or not?"

"If it wouldn't be breaching any rules about client confidentiality."

She was teasing me, but I didn't mind. I was eager to have someone to share my brilliance with. I wanted her to know I'd become a detective, to be my corroborating witness. I grabbed the packet of photos off the kitchen counter, plopped myself down on the couch next to her, and spread the pictures out on the table.

"I've laid these out in chronological order," I said. "Take a look and tell me what you see."

She took her feet off the table and leaned forward. "Is there something to see?"

"If you know where to look."

She examined the pictures, then gave me a disapproving look. "You're not talking about her nipples, are you?"

"I'm only interested in what's pertinent to the case," I said, trying to sound offended and superior at the same time. "Try and focus."

"You're serious about this."

I handed her the magnifying glass. "Why wouldn't I be?"

Carol took the magnifying glass and leaned over the photos again. "Because you've never been serious about anything else before."

I didn't think that was true, and I wasn't quite sure how to take the comment.

"She's obviously got money," Carol said, still scrutinizing the pictures. "Aside from the car, the clothes, and the jewelry, she's had a lot of work done."

"What work?" I asked like I already knew.

"Her nose, her eyes, her chin," Carol replied.

No wonder Lauren looked sculpted to me. I'd have to learn to listen to myself. I was more observant than I thought.

"Maybe even her breasts, too," she added, "mainly because I hate to think anyone was born that way."

"That's the obvious stuff," I said. "The real story is more subtle."

I was enjoying the hell out of this and feeling very smart. Because if Carol hadn't spotted it yet, and I considered her a lot more intelligent than me, then my deduction must really have been clever.

She smiled at me.

I'd never seen a smile like that on Carol before. It was as if she was intrigued and amused and surprised all at once.

"You're sure pleased with yourself. That's a first, too," she said. "Why don't you just tell me, and save me the hard work and suspense."

So I did. I showed her that Lauren wore a gold necklace, tiny earrings, and her wedding ring during her day at the beach. She was also wearing them when she went to Beverly Hills Collateral Lenders—but she was only wearing her wedding ring when she came out.

"Lauren hocked her jewelry," I concluded. "The question now is *why?* Debts? Drugs? Blackmail?"

"Collagen? Botox? Lipo?"

Carol smiled. I gave her a chastising look, or at least my best shot at one.

"You're not helping," I said. "I'm trying to work here."

She looked at me, as if she'd just noticed a giant mole on my cheek or something. "You are, aren't you? I mean, you really do want to find out what is going on."

"Of course I do. It's my job."

"You know something, Harvey? You may have stumbled into your true calling."

"You think so?" I wanted to believe she was right.

Instead of answering me, she did something totally unexpected.

She kissed me hard on the lips and thrust her hand inside my bathrobe. I forgot all about my calling and answered a new one.

Chapter Seven

$$\diamondsuit \quad \diamondsuit \quad \diamondsuit$$

I guess something I learned from *Mannix* was true. Being a private eye really is an aphrodisiac to women. Carol had never attacked me like that before.

I'm afraid the surprise and excitement were too much, because I came in about three minutes. But I don't think Carol minded; it calmed me down and allowed me to concentrate real hard on getting her off. And believe me, it took my complete attention. Pleasing a woman, especially Carol, isn't easy and with me, at least, there's a lot of potential for embarrassment and humiliation.

She rewarded me for all my hard work with a nice, squealing, writhing orgasm that nearly broke my nose on her pubic bone, but I didn't mind. I even jumped in, literally, to enjoy the last few squeals of it with her.

It was so dark, and things happened so fast, she never saw my cuts and bruises, so she mistook my occasional groans of pain for pleasure.

Carol fell right to sleep afterwards.

Between the sex, the pain, and the things on my mind, I didn't get as much sleep as I would have liked. But I get laid so rarely, I'm willing to sacrifice just about anything for it, especially sleep, when I usually dream about having sex anyway.

Around eleven, I slipped out of bed, took four Advils, smeared a lot of Arrid Extra Dry under my arms to hide the smell of sex on me, and got into my clean uniform. I grabbed some fresh clothes, gathered up the photos, and left as quickly as I could.

To be honest, I was eager to get out of there. I was confused and more than a little bit ashamed and thought that leaving the apartment would change things.

It didn't.

I just couldn't understand why it had happened. Not the sex with Carol, that was great. It was what happened *during* the sex, and it was all I could think about afterward.

What was troubling me was this: when I was making love to Carol, it was Lauren that I saw.

The first thing I did when I got in the shack was check the surveillance tapes to reassure myself that Lauren Parkus didn't leave between the time I abandoned my post and her husband came home.

She hadn't.

The rest of the night I just watched TV, stared into the darkness, and guzzled Cokes to stay awake. I tried not to think about Lauren Parkus, or why I saw her while making love to Carol, or why I felt so guilty about it. So, naturally, that was all I thought about.

I figured there weren't many men who could look at Lauren Parkus and not fantasize a little bit about her, especially while having sex. But that didn't make me feel any better.

In fact, by seven forty-five a.m. when Cyril Parkus came down, I was so wired on caffeine and so afraid he'd guess I was horny for his wife that my hands were shaking.

He rolled down the window of his Jag and looked up at

me. "Anything new, Harvey?"

"I'm afraid there is, Mr. Parkus." I handed him the packet of photos, my handwritten report, and receipts for the film developing, parking, and overpriced muffin. I'd left out certain photos, I'm pretty sure you can guess which ones.

"Your wife hocked her jewelry in Beverly Hills," I said as he flipped through the photos.

Parkus stopped at the picture of her going into the Collateral Lender and shook his head in disagreement. "She'll go anywhere for a bargain. How do you know she didn't just go in there to shop?"

I was hoping he'd ask, so I could show off. "You'll notice she's wearing her jewelry when she goes in and not when she comes out. Ergo, she hocked it."

He looked at those two pictures again, then back at me. His eyes were cold.

"Ergo, Harvey?"

I met his gaze, just to prove I had some balls, and wouldn't always take his shit.

"Ergo, Mr. Parkus."

He must have seen something in my eyes besides my lack of sleep, and if he did see something, I wished he'd held up a mirror so I could've seen it, too.

Parkus blinked and turned back to the pictures. "Lauren doesn't need to hock anything, Harvey. She has plenty of money."

"Maybe she doesn't want you to know what she's spending it on." I pressed my advantage. "How much was the jewelry worth?"

"About thirty thousand, give or take." He stuffed the pictures back into their envelope.

"Any idea what she'd need that kind of money for?"

57

"If I did, I wouldn't need you, would I?" He tossed the envelope back to me and drove off without waiting for my reply.

It's nice to be needed, especially at one hundred fifty dollars a day plus expenses.

I almost slept through the most important day in the investigation.

If Lauren Parkus hadn't been in such a hurry coming out of the gate at ten a.m., and if she hadn't cut off a Lincoln, and if the old geezer driving it hadn't honked at her long and loud to show how angry he was, I wouldn't have woken up. I'd have still been sitting there waiting for her to come out when she came home later that afternoon.

But the guy did honk, I woke up, and I was able to follow her. We headed south again on the Ventura Freeway, getting off in Calabasas and taking Malibu Canyon towards the sea.

It's a real nice drive through the Santa Monica Mountains, with lots of charred trees and blackened earth from the annual wildfires to look at. You also pass some dramatic gouges and gashes in the hillside from the seasonal mudslides. It's not the place I'd pick to build my secluded mansion, but I'm not a rich movie star or studio executive.

When we hit the Pacific Coast Highway, she turned left towards Santa Monica, traveling south along the beaches.

It's amazing how beautiful the ocean is, especially when you consider it's just a giant toilet that's been used by millions of people and never been flushed. There's only a few months out of the year when stepping in it is actually hazardous to your health. The rest of the time, you'll just get a rash that we let the tourists think is sunburn. But despite its variable toxicity, the sea along the Southern California coastline is always nice to look at and that's got to count for something.

Lauren took the off-ramp up to Ocean Avenue, but instead of going into Santa Monica, she surprised me by making a hard left onto the Pier.

I was surprised for a lot of reasons, but mainly because it was such a cliché. Once again, *Mannix* got it right, or maybe we just can't help but imitate it. Maybe the clichés and conventions are so ingrained, they've become instinctive behavior.

In old TV cop shows, people are always having their clandestine meetings in decrepit warehouses and abandoned amusement parks. I guess since most of the decrepit warehouses in LA were converted to soundstages, and the last abandoned amusement park was paved over decades ago, the Santa Monica Pier was the perfect compromise.

Beyond the landmark carousel, the Pier has all the allure of one of those traveling carnivals that set up for a weekend or two in a vacant field or shopping center parking lot. The big attractions are a Ferris wheel, a rinky-dink roller coaster, and a noisy pinball arcade where old Pac-Man machines go to die.

I didn't know much about Lauren Parkus, but I was willing to bet she hadn't picked this spot, which already told me a lot about the person she was going to meet. Whoever he was, he wasn't in her class.

He was in mine.

Lauren paid the ten bucks and parked behind the arcade and near the ticket booth for the rides. I parked two rows over, across from her, so I could see her face. She sat in her car for a moment, looking at the line of weary Hispanic nannies waiting for tickets, pushing elaborate strollers full of plump, white kids dribbling drool and snot onto their

Izod polo shirts and Guess overalls.

I wondered what she was thinking and snapped a few pictures on the chance I might see the answer on her face later, under a magnifying glass.

After a few moments, Lauren put on a pair of sunglasses and got out, carrying a large purse. She'd dressed down for this, wearing jeans and a big, untucked blouse loosely buttoned over a blue T-shirt.

She walked slowly and deliberately towards the rides and I followed a few yards behind, trying to look inconspicuous, which wasn't easy without a kid, a stroller, or a date. I pretended to take pictures, like I was a tourist who loved seedy amusement parks.

I was pretty excited, and nervous, too, because I could feel that I was coming up on the big moment I'd been waiting for, the key revelation in the case. But I was hoping it wouldn't be the end, but rather send things in a new direction. I was enjoying this job too much for it to finish so soon.

As I moved through the crowd, I kept my eye open for thugs from the Syndicate, European hitmen, and Ninja assassins, because that's what Joe Mannix would do. I wasn't sure what I'd do if I spotted any of them, though, since, unlike Mannix, I don't carry a gun and hadn't been in a fistfight since the fourth grade. Luckily for me, they seemed to be busy elsewhere that day.

She took a seat at a table in front of a hot dog place. A moment later, a guy sat down across from her and she seemed to recoil. I couldn't blame her.

He looked like the kind of character Martin Sheen used to play on *Cannon* and *Barnaby Jones* before he became the President of the United States on TV. The guy had a thick, bushy mustache on his thin face that hung over his leering grin and must've got stuck in everything he ate. His deep-set eyes and sunken cheeks made him look older than he probably was, which I pegged at around thirty-four. He let the stringy, black hair on the back of his head grow over his shoulders in a botched attempt to make you forget his receding hairline.

She wasn't fucking this guy, I was certain of that. Her whole body screamed out her repulsion. He had this relaxed, cocky air about him. I wanted to beat the shit out of the guy and I didn't even know him.

I snapped a bunch of pictures and, since I couldn't hear what they were saying, I tried to read their expressions and body language instead. It was like watching one of those soap operas on the Spanish channel.

I could tell she was angry, but pleading at the same time. He was enjoying himself way too much. He liked looking at her, but he liked torturing her even more, which is why I knew even before she gave him the bulging envelope from her purse that this was about blackmail.

The package was a half-filled manila envelope folded over itself and taped together that I guessed held about thirty thousand dollars.

He stuck the money inside his shirt, said something, and grinned.

"You promised!" she yelled in fury, startling me.

But he didn't even flinch. He kissed the air between them, stood up, and strode off, relaxed and happy with himself.

Lauren Parkus stayed there, staring at the space where he'd been, tears streaming from beneath her dark, impenetrable glasses.

Chapter Eight

$$\diamond \quad \diamond \quad \diamond$$

I was right about food getting stuck in his mustache. From where I sat, a couple tables away from him in the food court of the Santa Monica Place mall, I could see the grains of fried rice getting trapped in the tangle above his lip as he stuffed himself with Chinese food.

Back on the pier, I had five seconds to choose between staying with Lauren or following her blackmailer. I figured since her business was done, I wouldn't miss anything if I left her.

Lauren's blackmailer strode up the pier to the mall, patting his stomach every so often to feel the thirty grand underneath his shirt. I'd probably have done the same thing, if I was him. As soon as he was in the mall, he went straight to the food court and got himself the three ninety-nine combo plate at the Wok Inn.

As long as I was there, I bought myself a slice of pizza and a Coke, got a table where I could see him, and thought about things. I wondered what he had on Lauren, and if there were pictures or recordings somewhere that Cyril Parkus might pay me to get back. And if I did get hired to do it, I wondered how the hell I'd pull it off.

Things were getting complicated and scary and exciting,

words I never could have used before to describe my life. I liked it.

He finished his lunch and got up without bussing his table. I thought about snagging his fork for fingerprints, but I realized I didn't have an irascible friend on The Force to run them for me. I made a mental note to myself: if I stayed in this business, I'd have to cultivate a love-hate relationship with a police officer right away.

The blackmailer crossed Broadway, then walked down to the corner of Second Street and disappeared. I waited a minute, shoved the camera in my pants pocket, then ran across the street. I hurried up to the corner and peered around the edge of the building, just in time to see him enter the municipal parking structure, where you get the first three hours free. This guy and I had at least one thing in common. If I had the choice, I would have saved the ten bucks and parked there, too, even if I knew I'd be coming back to the car with thirty thousand dollars.

I jogged up to the parking structure, and when I got there, he was just stepping into the elevator, leaving me with a split-second choice to make. I could either go in the elevator with him, or run up the stairs and somehow try to meet him at whatever floor he stopped at. It wasn't that hard a choice to make.

I rushed into the elevator.

He grabbed me as I came in, threw me back against the wall, and slammed his fist into my stomach. I keeled over, grasping at his shirt as I went down, pulling it out of his pants. The packet of money hit the floor just before I did.

I ended up face-down on the floor, mouth open wide, unable to breathe, clutching my stomach, my body on top of his money. I was panicked. It wasn't the pain as much as it was the shock and the inability to breathe.

That's when he started kicking me in the ribs, again and again, screaming, "Get up! Get up you motherfucker!"

I wanted to say, "If you'll stop kicking me, I will," but I couldn't breathe, much less form words. With each kick, I imagined bones shattering and internal organs bursting like water balloons. That's what it felt like. He was killing me.

His foot must have finally got sore, or he got bored, because he stopped kicking me, grabbed me by my shirt, and rolled me over.

He hesitated for a moment, then picked up his money, scowling with disgust, holding it by its edges. The envelope was soiled with big, wet stains.

"Shit, you pissed all over my money!"

I wasn't surprised. Somewhere between the punch and the third kick, I'd lost all control of my body. I was just a lump of pain and misery and I wanted to die.

"What the fuck's the matter with you?" He kicked me sharply in the balls. I didn't think I could hurt any more than I already did. I was wrong. It was a tsunami of pain that swamped my entire body, from my groin to the tips of the individual hairs on my head. "What am I supposed to do with money that smells like piss?"

I gagged and began to choke on my undigested pizza. I imagine Spenser would have had a wittier answer. He probably wouldn't have started crying.

I did.

He glared at me with utter fury, breathing hard, his chin trembling. It's hard work kicking a guy when he's down.

"You can tell her this is what I'll do to her face, if I ever see you or anybody else on my ass again."

He lifted his foot back to give me a good kick in the face, one that would flatten my nose against the inside of my skull, and I closed my eyes, like that would actually give me any protection.

I heard a ding and felt nothing. I opened my eyes to blurrily see him shoving his way past a shocked family of six standing outside the elevator doors.

"The queer grabbed my balls," he said by way of explanation.

"We'll take the stairs, Martha," the father told his family, hustling them away from me. I would have thanked them for their help if I'd been able to speak. Just by being there, they saved my face.

With the beating finished, I managed to suck in some air and cough out some puke. It cleared my vision enough for me to clearly see the number eight on a pillar outside, and to realize I was on the eighth floor. It would take the black-mailer some time to drive down to the street.

Now, this is when a very weird thing happened. My pre-historic monkey brain, the part of our minds that's un-changed from the caveman days, must have been hardwired for detective work. I should have been curled up in a fetal position in my puddle of piss, puke, and tears, whimpering for help. Instead, I reached up and hit the button for the first floor, pain ricocheting around inside of me. The doors closed and my arm dropped. I felt the elevator descending. I willed myself to pull out my camera from my pocket and slid myself around to face the door.

When the doors opened, I dragged myself out on my stomach, propped the camera in front of me on the pave-ment, aimed the lens at the aisle, and waited for the black-mailer to drive down. I prayed the camera hadn't been broken by one of his kicks.

A moment or two later, he came screeching by in a new Ford Focus. I don't think he saw me. I managed to snap one or two pictures before he sped past on his way to the cashier. I hoped I got his license plate, though I had no idea what I would do with the information.

I was still there, soaked in my own urine and bile, when the family of six came out of the stairwell. They pretended not to see me. So did the lovely young couple that walked up five minutes later. They just stepped over me and got in the elevator, then immediately got out and stepped over me again to take the stairs instead.

It took me a good ten minutes before I'd gathered enough oxygen, and enough courage, to try sitting up. The pain was like a fresh kick, but at least I could breathe. Sort of. Each breath was like being stuck with knives. I'd broken a few ribs playing touch football in high school, and it felt just like this.

I propped myself up against the wall and sat there, clutching my sides, gathering strength, waiting for my pants to dry, and hoping the pain would wane.

More people passed me on their way to the elevator and tried not to look at me. I think if I hadn't wet myself, I would have gotten more sympathy. As it was, I was written off as another one of Santa Monica's ubiquitous homeless people.

Next time I took a beating, I would work harder at controlling my bladder. Next time, I wouldn't cry, either.

Yes, I was thinking about the next time.

Because as miserable as I felt, as humiliated as I was, as much pain as I was in, I was elated.

I had just gotten my first professional beating.

Someone had just pounded the piss out of me because my investigation had gotten me too close. It didn't matter that my bungled surveillance was what got me in that elevator and got me thrashed. Nor did it matter that I didn't even get in a punch of my own. With each kick, he acknowledged that I was on a case and I was a threat to him.

It was no different from Syndicate thugs trying to run over Jim Rockford. Or a hired sniper taking a shot at Dan Tana. Or someone waiting in Travis McGee's houseboat to ambush him.

I was one of them now. I wasn't simply a detective. I was Harvey Mapes, private eye.

I may have considered myself a private dick, but as I sat in my car stripping off my piss-soaked pants and underwear, I certainly didn't feel like a sex machine to all the chicks.

I left my soiled clothes on the pier, rolled down the window, and drove back to the Valley naked from the waist down, hoping to air myself out a little. I figured if anyone could see I was half-naked, they were too damn close to my car anyway.

I decided against going to the ER. I knew I had a few broken ribs, but a doctor wouldn't do anything for me I couldn't do myself, besides prescribe some strong pain-killers. I would have to make do with handfuls of Advils, which I could buy in bulk from Costco for what a pharmacist charged for two pills of something fancier.

After I dropped off my film for developing, I'd buy some Ace bandages and a big jug of Pepto-Bismol, since eating Advils like M&Ms ravages your stomach. The only thing more humiliating than a detective who pisses his pants is one who can't be more than five feet away from a toilet for fear he'll shit himself.

I got off the freeway at the Ventura Boulevard exit and parked behind the first gas station I saw. I put on my uniform, got out of the car, and limped into the men's room. Those simple actions hurt more than I can describe. Suffice it to say that every move I made was painful, so I won't belabor the point from now on. Take it as a given.

I shoved my blood-and-puke-stained shirt in the trash, washed my face in the sink, and took a pee to see if there was any blood in my urine. There wasn't, which I took to mean there wasn't any internal bleeding, not that I had the slightest bit of medical knowledge.

Still, I was relieved.

I got back in the car and drove to the Thrifty on the way to my place, dropping the film off at their one-hour photo counter. I bought my medical supplies and went to my apartment.

As soon as I got home, I stripped and showered. After that, I wrapped the Ace bandages tightly around my waist, washed down six Advils with a couple gulps of Pepto-Bismol, and lay down on my bed to rest for a few minutes.

I awoke to pounding in my head from inside and out.

The apartment was dark. Pain pulsed in my head, keeping time with the sound of a fist banging on my front door.

I sat up slowly, pleased that the tight bandages were providing some support and a slight easing of my pain.

I put on my bathrobe and dragged myself to the front door. I could have stayed where I was and yelled to Carol to stop her damn knocking, but I was afraid it would hurt me more than walking across the apartment.

I unlocked the door and swung it open.

"Oh my God, what happened to you?" Carol said as she came in, closing the door behind her.

"Nothing," I said. "I'd love to talk, but I got some errands to run before I go to work."

"Harvey, it's after midnight." She turned on the light. "I just got back from the movies."

"Shit!" I yelled, and confirmed my earlier fears. Yelling *did* hurt more than walking across the room. I clutched myself and wanted to cry. I'd slept over ten hours.

I wasn't so concerned about being late to work; Clay would cover for me. But Thrifty was closed now, which meant I wouldn't be able to pick up the pictures until after my shift Saturday morning. I'd have nothing to show Cyril Parkus. I put both hands on the kitchen counter and groaned. Now I felt like a failure. This hurt worse than the beating.

Carol turned the light off again.

"Why did you do that?" I asked.

"Because right now you look a lot better in the dark." She came up behind me and tenderly caressed my back. She'd never touched me like that before. "Are you going to tell me what happened?"

"Maybe tomorrow," I said. "I have to go to work."

"You're in no condition to work."

"You could be in a coma and do my job," I said and shuffled off to the bedroom.

"Then you're certainly qualified," she replied.

I was changing carefully into my uniform when Carol came into the bedroom and, without saying a word, helped me put on my pants and button my shirt. It was the most intimate moment of my adult life. For some reason I couldn't figure out, I wanted to cry, but I brought all my manly resources to bear and controlled myself. When she was done, she gave me a quick kiss on the cheek.

In the glow of my clock radio, I could see the concern on her face when she spoke.

"I'll be waiting for you tomorrow."

And I knew, no matter what, she would be.

Chapter Nine

$$\diamond \quad \diamond \quad \diamond$$

It was after one a.m. by the time I got to Bel Vista Estates with some burgers from McDonald's for Clay and me. Clay took one look at me and offered to work the next shift in my place, but I told him I needed the money.

I also told him I'd been mugged, which is why I looked like shit.

He asked me where it happened, and when I told him it was in a parking structure, he demanded to know which one, so he could scope it out for a redesign to enhance safety.

After Clay left, I checked the surveillance tapes. Lauren came home around two Friday afternoon and didn't come out again. I wasn't surprised.

I spent the rest of the night swallowing Advils, guzzling Pepto-Bismol, and going over the events of the previous day in my mind.

I wondered how he discovered that I was following him. As much as I tried, I couldn't isolate the fuck-up, maybe because it wasn't just one thing, but my entire performance. Maybe I was the fuck-up.

I wondered why he was driving a brand new Ford Focus, which didn't strike me as his kind of car, not that I knew him that well. I knew his foot pretty good, though, and it seemed like it belonged in a pickup truck or a used Firebird.

I wondered how he knew Lauren Parkus and what he could know about her that she was afraid of.

And I wondered how I would find him so I could do to him what he did to me.

By sunrise, I didn't have any better understanding than I did before, but I promised myself that by the end of the day, I would.

It would require a radical change in approach. So far, all I'd been doing was following people. So I decided that today, on my day off, I would blaze a trail of my own.

"Jesus Christ, Harvey, you're a security officer," *Sergeant* Victor Banos said after I told him what I told Clay. "You should have been able to take the guy."

"He caught me by surprise."

"You still should have taken him," Victor said. "I would have taken him. I know how to handle myself."

"I bet you do," I said. "Probably half a dozen times a day, too."

"You're a worthless piece of shit, Mapes. You don't deserve to wear the badge."

"It's not a badge," I said, "it's a patch."

"What's the fucking difference?"

I walked out before he could humiliate me any further. I was almost at my car when Cyril Parkus drove out of the gate and came up beside me in his wife's Range Rover.

"What happened to you, Harvey?" Parkus asked.

That question was becoming my theme song. It was a shame Sammy Davis, Jr. wasn't around any more to do the vocals.

"I took the elevator when I should have taken the stairs,"

I replied. "Look, Mr. Parkus, I don't have anything to tell you right now."

"What do you mean?" he snapped. "She did *something* yesterday, and I want to know what it was. That's what I paid you for."

"Your wife is being blackmailed," I replied. "If you give me a few hours, I can tell you who's doing it and maybe even why. Just stay close to her today; don't let her leave the house alone. Then come up with an excuse to meet me at Denny's around six."

He studied me for a long moment. "I hope you know what the fuck you're doing, Harvey."

So did I. Because at that precise moment, watching him make a U-turn and drive back up to the house, I didn't have the slightest idea how I was going to pull off what I'd just promised.

I rushed back to Thrifty in Northridge and went through the photos right there at the counter.

Even with Lauren's eyes hidden by her sunglasses, her anger and her fear still came through, maybe even stronger than it did when I saw her on the Pier. Pictures are funny that way.

I pulled out my magnifying glass and studied the guy who kicked my ass, hoping to spot a tattoo or fraternal ring or something else I might use to find out who he was. No such luck.

I'd have to rely on the license plate and come up with some scam to get the DMV to spit out his name and address for me.

In theory, anyway, that was a good idea. What I really needed was a plugged-in techno-buddy who could hack into anything anywhere. Just about every private eye, secret agent, and suave adventurer has a buddy like that these days.

My buddy could have a name like Joe "Hard Drive" Hardigan.

But I didn't have a buddy like that yet.

I also didn't have a picture of the license plate. I had a picture of the back tires and a chunk of the car's bumper.

There was something on the bumper, though, that caught my eye. I looked at it under the magnifying glass. It was a tiny green sticker, a stylish rendering of the letter "S" and a code number underneath: "UC2376."

It looked familiar to me, but I couldn't place where I'd seen it before. I figured it was a parking permit of some kind, but from where? The UC could stand for the University of California, and could come from any of their campuses statewide, though the guy who beat me up didn't look like a student to me.

The sticker could also be a parking permit for a factory, an office building, a government office, or even a gated community like the one I guarded. The possibilities were endless.

As I walked outside to my car, it occurred to me again how unusual I thought it was for the blackmailer to be driving a new Ford Focus, a practical economy car. It's the last car a guy like that would buy.

So I decided to assume that the car wasn't his.

Which meant it could be stolen, though if you're gonna steal a car, it would be something nicer than a Ford Focus, even if all you were gonna do with it was take a joyride. There's no joy in riding in a Ford Focus, believe me.

If I assumed it wasn't stolen, that he'd borrowed it, then maybe it belonged to his employer. Perhaps the sticker meant it was a fleet car of some kind.

And then it hit me, just as I reached my little Kia Sephia. It was a rental car.

Right away, I knew my deduction was right. I knew it because it matched the evidence, it was logical, and it fit my astute observations of his character.

And I knew it because the tiny green sticker on his bumper was the same as the one on my car.

The lady behind the counter at the Swift Rent-A-Car office on Ventura Boulevard looked like she'd been manufactured at the same plant where they make stewardesses, bank tellers, telephone operators, and Barbie dolls.

She was blond, blue-eyed, and her body had all the right measurements so she could fit into her pre-tailored, green rent-a-car gal uniform. I was hoping she'd be just as robotic and predictable as her appearance promised.

"May I help you?" she chirped.

I strode up in a new polo shirt and khakis I bought at K-Mart.

"My name is John D. MacDonald, and I'm a best-selling author of mystery novels. I'm doing some research for my next book, and I was hoping you could help me with a technical question about the rental car industry."

I said it all quickly, in a nervous blurt, just the way I'd memorized it. I also whipped out a new paperback reprint of *Nightmare in Pink* and held it in front of me like an ID.

"What does the D stand for?" she asked.

"Excuse me?"

I wasn't prepared for improvisation. I'd come up with a very detailed script, and already she was deviating from her part.

"The D," she repeated. "People don't usually mention their middle initial unless they are very proud of it."

"What about Captain James T. Kirk? He tells everybody about his middle initial, even aliens who don't understand English and certainly don't give a damn."

"Tiberius."

"Excuse me?"

"That's what his T stands for," she explained. "Would you like to know what Doctor McCoy's middle name was?"

"Actually, what I'd like to know is what this means." I handed her the photo of the blackmailer's bumper.

"What for?" she asked.

"My hero, Travis McGee, is tossed out of a car. And just before he passes out on the road, he sees that sticker with the logo and number. I was wondering what he could deduce from that clue."

"He didn't know the people in the car?"

"No," I replied testily, "they were thugs."

"What about the license plate?" she said. "Wouldn't he look at that, instead of a tiny bumper sticker?"

"There are no plates."

"Weren't the thugs worried that by driving around without plates, a cop might pull them over while they're holding McGee hostage?"

"They are on a rural country road where there are no cops."

"They didn't have to drive on other roads first to get to the rural road?"

"No."

She shrugged. "I'd rethink the whole situation, if I were you. It doesn't sound too plausible to me."

"Could you please just tell me what the numbers on the sticker mean?"

"The first three characters identify the rental location," she said. "The remaining numbers identify the vehicle."

"So what, for instance, could you tell me about this car?"

"Whose car is it?"

"I don't know, that's why I'm asking you," I replied angrily without thinking. An instant later, I realized my mistake and hurried to repair it. "I took this picture of a stranger's car as research. I'm trying to go through the same steps my hero would."

"You going to jump out of a car, too?"

"I already have." I lifted my shirt to show her the bruises and bandaging. "As you can see, I take my research very seriously. I'd really appreciate your help."

She smiled now, the first genuine smile since I walked in the door.

"The car came from our rental desk at the Universal Sheraton," she replied. "The UC stands for Universal City."

There's no real city there, just the Universal Studios Tour. The blackmailer must have decided to do a little sightseeing while he was here. Since LA has no real sights, you have to go someplace where they manufacture them.

"What can you tell me about who rented the car?"

"Nothing," she said.

"Because you don't have the information, or because you just don't want to tell me?"

"Because it's confidential."

"So, you have the information."

"Yes," she replied.

"So, it would be possible for my hero to get it."

"I don't see how," she said.

"What if, for instance, he seduced the woman behind the counter?"

"You gonna try that as research, too?" she asked.

"Would it work?" I replied.

"No chance in hell, John D.," she replied.

I smiled. "What if I told you what the D stood for?"
I also wasn't beyond begging.

"Dann," she said. "That's with two Ns."

"Excuse me?"

"That's what the D is for," she said. "He wrote twenty-one Travis McGee novels before his death in 1986. My dad was a big fan, though I never understood that 'wounded bird' crap."

I felt like I'd just been kicked in the ribs again.

"If you knew I wasn't John D. MacDonald, why did you help me?"

"I wasn't going to, until you lifted your shirt."

"Thanks," I tossed her the book and walked out. I was almost out the door, when I paused for effect, then turned around.

"Horatio," I said.

"Excuse me?"

"That's Doctor McCoy's middle name."

And with that I smiled and walked out, feeling pretty cool.

I knew watching all that TV would pay off someday. My good mood lasted all the way until I got to my car.

I still didn't know who the blackmailer was. All I knew was that he rented his car at the Universal Sheraton. So, I figured, odds were that was where the guy was staying.

But what the hell was I going to do now?

I thought about it a minute. Spenser would walk the parking structure until he found the car, then he'd find a place to hide out and wait. When the blackmailer came for his car, Spenser would beat him up and make him talk.

I was in no condition to do that now.

I was in no condition to do that *before* my beating.

So, I asked myself what Jim Rockford would do.

I stopped by Target before going to the Universal Sheraton and bought a hammer, a gym bag, and a red sweatsuit.

I visited a gas station, went into the restroom, and changed into my uniform again; then I put the red sweatsuit on over it.

I went back to the car and drove to Universal Studios, not the part in the Valley where they make movies, but the amusement park, hotels, and shopping center above it, on the hills along the Cahuenga Pass.

I was lucky the blackmailer wasn't staying at Disneyland, or the task ahead of me would have been a lot harder. They've got more hotels there, thousands of guests, and tighter security.

I paid seven dollars and fifty cents to park in the tour lot, then walked down the hill and across the street to the Sheraton's parking structure.

It took me two hours of wandering through the five-story parking structure before I finally found it. The Ford Focus was parked near the stairwell on the third floor. The bumper sticker matched the one in my photo.

I double-checked it against the photo a couple times to make absolutely sure, then I looked around. I didn't see anyone or any security cameras and I was fairly certain there wasn't going to be a car alarm in a rented Ford Focus. So I grabbed the hammer from the gym bag on my shoulder, took one more look, and then smashed the passenger's side window of the car.

I was right, the Ford Focus didn't have a car alarm. But every other car within twenty yards did, and they were wailing. The alarms echoed off the concrete walls, amplifying the sound a hundred-fold and turning the entire parking structure into a loudspeaker.

After the events of the last two days, I was developing a serious hatred of parking structures.

I quickly reached into the Ford, opened the glove compartment, and grabbed the rental agreement, which was nicely folded inside a pamphlet-sized, Swift Rent-A-Car folder. I shoved the folder and the hammer in my bag and ran for the stairwell.

Running is something you generally want to avoid when you've got an unknown number of broken ribs. It is extraordinarily painful. But the alarms panicked me. So did the sight of two security guards in a golf cart speeding down the ramp from the upper floor.

I say they were speeding, because for the last few days I'd been driving a Kia Sephia, and compared to it, a golf cart is a formula one racer.

I'm not much of a runner even without broken ribs, so I knew I couldn't outrun them. As soon as I got in the stairwell, I peeled off my sweatsuit and shoved it in the trash, which left me in my security guard uniform. I stuck the picture and the folder in my shirt and ditched the gym bag, too. Then I ran the rest of the way down the stairs.

The instant I hit the street, I fell to the ground, clutching my sides. It was part of my plan to do that, but my performance was helped greatly by the fact I was in tremendous pain and too dizzy to stand. Not having to actually act when you're supposed to be acting makes you a lot more convincing.

A few moments later one security guard burst out of the stairwell, and another sped out of the exit ramp in the golf cart. The one from the stairs rushed up to me.

"You looking for a guy in a red sweatsuit?" I rasped.

"Yeah, you see him?" the guard asked.

What a stupid question, I thought. That guard would be a sergeant in no time.

"He tackled me like a linebacker and ran into the structure across the street."

"You gonna be okay?"

I nodded. "Just get the son-of-a-bitch."

The guard mumbled something into a walkie-talkie, jumped into his buddy's golf cart, and scooted across the street in hot pursuit.

When I drove down the hill fifteen minutes later, now dressed in my polo shirt and wearing sunglasses, the entrances and exits to the structure across from the hotel were blocked by private security patrol cars.

I smiled to myself and wiped tears from my eyes. The smile was from pride, the tears were from the pain. But it was worth it.

Now I knew who the blackmailer was.

Chapter Ten

$\diamond$ $\diamond$ $\diamond$

I arrived at Denny's early to prepare my report, calculate my bill, and rehearse my presentation. I was impressed with myself and was pretty sure Mr. Parkus would share my opinion, once he learned the results of my work.

Sure, I'd made a few mistakes along the way, but there's a learning curve to any new job. The fact was, despite a car accident and a serious beating, I'd still managed to pull off what he'd hired me to do, and then some. And now I felt I was ready to take on the next phase of the operation: uncovering Lauren's secret and retrieving whatever evidence the blackmailer had.

I told the waitress to start defrosting the steaks. There was going to be some big dining tonight.

Cyril Parkus showed up right on time, wearing jeans and a Ralph Lauren sweatshirt, which I guessed he picked up at the outlet mall for fifty dollars. I thought about telling him he could buy five sweatshirts just like it, only without the horse on the chest, for the same price at the JCPenney outlet in Woodland Hills. Then again, I figured the horse was probably worth forty bucks to him, so I kept quiet.

"We've got to make this fast, Harvey," he said as he slid into the booth. "I told Lauren I was going to make a quick run down to the grocery store for a bottle of wine."

"This won't take long," I replied, and laid out in front of him my handwritten report with receipts stapled to it. "Here's my report, my bill, and my expenses. Don't bother reading it now, I'll give you the headlines. Your wife went down to the Santa Monica Pier yesterday morning and paid thirty thousand dollars to this man."

I dealt the pictures to him like playing cards.

He picked up the best shot of the blackmailer and jerked as if he'd been hit with defibrillator paddles. The blood drained from his face. His eyes widened and he swallowed hard. Parkus did everything except spontaneously combust.

So, I asked, "Do you know the guy?"

"Nope," he lied.

I decided right then that I had to play poker with this guy some day.

"Maybe this will help," I said. "His name is Arlo Pelz. Does that mean anything to you?"

"No," he lied again, staring at the picture.

"He's staying at the Universal Sheraton, but I don't know for how long."

Parkus just nodded and took a drink of my water. "You got anything more?"

Unfortunately, the only information in the rental agreement was the guy's name, his credit card receipt, and how much he was paying per day for the car. Arlo didn't pay the extra few bucks for insurance. That was a mistake.

"That's it for now," I replied. "But I'm just getting started."

"That won't be necessary." Parkus shook his head and gathered up the photos. "You've done a really great job."

I couldn't believe what I was hearing. Parkus wanted me to stop. He wanted me to leave the mystery unsolved and go back to being a security guard.

"But there's still a lot we don't know," I whined. I didn't mean for it to come out that way, but it did. "I mean, this could be the first payment or the fifth. Who knows how long this has been going on—"

"I'll take it from here, Harvey," he interrupted.

Parkus reached into his pocket, pulled out his money clip, and peeled out ten one-hundred-dollar bills. "This should cover what I owe and a little bit more as a bonus."

"But I still have to find out who Pelz is, where he came from, and get whatever he has on Lauren."

He looked at me at the mention of her name, a strange expression on his face.

"Your wife," I corrected, but the damage was done.

"I appreciate everything you've done, Harvey." Parkus slid out of his seat, taking the pictures with him. "But I have the answers I wanted. I'm counting on you to keep our arrangement, and what you've found out, completely confidential."

"Don't worry," I said, unable to hide the disappointment from my voice. "I'm a professional."

He nodded and hurried out.

I watched him drive off in his Jag and then I looked down at the crisp one-hundred-dollar bills on the table.

I still didn't know who Arlo Pelz was, or why he was blackmailing Lauren, or what her secret was, or why it scared her. But there in front of me was a thousand bucks from a satisfied client.

If he didn't care, why should I?

I was officially a private detective now. There was the money to prove it. That should be enough for me.

I shoved the cash in my pocket and left. I could afford to eat at a nicer place.

★ ★ ★ ★ ★

I knocked on Carol's door around seven p.m. and asked her if she'd eaten yet. She said she hadn't.

"Then I want you to get dressed in something nice, pick a very fancy place to eat, make a reservation, and meet me here in thirty minutes."

"I can't afford it," she said.

"Did I ask you to pay?"

"You asked me to do everything else."

"I'm taking you out tonight."

She narrowed her eyes. "But I'm making all the arrangements."

"Right," I said. "Remember to pick someplace expensive."

I hurried off before she could ask me any more questions. I went back to my apartment to class myself up. I slathered some Arrid Extra Dry Ultra Fresh Gel under my arms, ran some water through my hair, and brushed my teeth. I washed down a couple Advils with a gulp of Pepto-Bismol, then realized I should have done that before I brushed my teeth. The Pepto leaves a chalky residue on your tongue, but it has a nice, minty scent, so I decided not to brush again.

I changed into the only suit I had. It was black; I bought it for my mother's funeral two years ago. That was the last time I wore it, but it still fit, and black is always cool.

Carol was waiting outside when I opened my door. She was wearing a low-cut dress, a fake-pearl necklace, and high-heeled shoes. She was also wearing make-up and had done something different to her hair that made her face seem bolder and sharper. Her eyes sparkled and her lips seemed fuller and redder than ever before.

She was beautiful.

Better than that, she'd become a woman.

Carol must have been thinking the same about me, opposite sex-wise, because she gave me the once-over two or three times and then flashed me this big smile.

"We've never gone out before," she said.

"We've gone out hundreds of times."

"Not like this."

I took her hand. "Then we should have."

The Bistro Garden in Studio City was big, open, and airy. The place was alive with the tinkle of silverware, soft music, and the occasional trill of a cell phone. It was fancy without being snobby.

Well, that's not entirely true. When I drove up in my Kia Sephia, the valet hesitated before opening Carol's door, like a compact car with a sticker price under twenty thousand dollars carries some kind of infectious disease. But she gave him a look through the window that promised immediate emasculation unless he jumped to attention, so he did. That was the only bump in an otherwise perfect evening.

While we waited for our steaks and lobsters, and ogled the movie stars and agents at the other tables, she took my hand from across the table.

"You're forgetting something," she said.

"Would you like some wine?" I replied. "Order whatever you like."

"Thank you, but that's not it. Last night, you promised me an explanation," she said. "I want to know what happened to you yesterday and what tonight is all about."

I thought about it for a minute. I thought about what I should leave out, what I should exaggerate, and what I should invent. In the end, I decided to tell her the truth and only leave out the part about wetting myself and everything related to that.

Even without that part, as I told the story I kept waiting to see the disappointment, disgust, and pity on her face, or for her to just start laughing at me. But instead she did something strange. She kept her hand on mine and, every so often, gave it a little squeeze.

Our dinner arrived, and while we ate, I told her the rest, about breaking into Pelz's car and presenting my case to Parkus and getting paid the bonus.

"I was right, Harvey," she said when I'd finished. "You're good at this."

"Even though I let Arlo Pelz beat me up?"

"The thing is you didn't give up; you stuck to it and succeeded in what you were hired to do."

I shrugged. "I suppose you're right."

"But more importantly, you proved something to yourself."

"I did?"

"It's changed everything about you. You're proud of yourself, maybe for the first time," she said. "Isn't that what we're here celebrating?"

I didn't really know what we were doing. I just knew I didn't want to eat dinner at Denny's and that I didn't want to be alone that night and there was only one person I really wanted to be with.

So, that's what I tried to tell her.

"I don't know what we're doing," I said. "I'm just glad we're doing it together."

Something seemed to melt in her. Me, too, if you want to know the truth.

Carol put her hand on mine. "Let's go home, Harvey."

It was the best sex of my life. It was like that moment

when she buttoned up my shirt, only with intercourse thrown in.

I don't know if it was because we had to go real slow because of my broken ribs, or because we'd dressed up nice and had a fancy dinner first, or because I'd finished a job and had some real money in my pocket.

All I know is that it lasted a long time, it felt real good, and afterwards I didn't want to be anywhere else but in her bed and in her arms.

So, why the hell couldn't I get Lauren Parkus out of my head?

I slipped out of bed, closed the door, and went into the kitchen. I picked up the phone, called the Universal Sheraton, and asked for Arlo Pelz's room.

It was after midnight, and I had no idea what I was going to say to him, so it was probably a good thing that he'd already checked out.

I hung up the phone and stood there for a moment in the dark before I realized Carol was standing in the bedroom doorway in her bathrobe, looking at me. A tomato would have been wearing my shirt and nothing else.

"What are you doing, Harvey?" she asked.

I'd actually been asking myself the same question.

"Nothing." I suddenly realized that I was naked and I wished I wasn't.

"You've been paid," Carol said. "The case is closed."

"I don't really feel like it is," I replied. "I don't know the answers to a lot of questions."

"The answers are none of your business."

"I know that, but I still want to know," I said. Now I saw the look of disappointment on her face that I'd been expecting before. "I'm just doing my job."

"No one is paying you anymore," she said.

No one ever paid Spenser, either—the Robert Urich TV Spenser, I mean. All that mattered was justice, honor, and duty. That duty was to solve the mystery. Hell, even Encyclopedia Brown always did that, regardless of whether or not somebody plunked a quarter down on his table.

"But I only did half the work," I said, trying to make her understand. "I didn't solve the mystery. I don't know who Arlo Pelz is or what Lauren Parkus is getting blackmailed about."

"You were hired to follow her and find out why she was acting strange. You did that. The client is happy and you got paid."

"Why do you think Cyril Parkus paid me so much? To buy me off. To get me to stop investigating. He knows who Pelz is."

"Then there's nothing left for you to investigate, is there? If he knows Pelz, then Parkus probably already knows what his wife's secret is, or if he doesn't, you gave him the leverage to get her to tell him."

She stood there, looking at me. I really wished I had some clothes on.

"This isn't about doing the job," Carol said. "It's about your curiosity."

"That's not true," I argued, feeling very exposed. I stepped behind the kitchen counter for some cover. "Maybe I can help her."

I was more exposed than I thought. I quickly corrected myself. "Maybe I can help *both* of them."

If she caught my slip, she didn't mention it.

"Harvey, you've done a good job. It could be the start of something. Of a lot of things. Don't screw it up now."

Carol turned around and went back to bed. I stood there for a moment, thinking about our conversation, weighing what she'd said. I also thought about what Spenser, Elvis Cole, Travis McGee, and Joe Mannix might say.

I knew what I had to do. I really didn't have any other choice.

I was parked down the street from the Bel Vista Estates gate by seven thirty the next morning.

I couldn't park in my usual spot, because *Sergeant* Victor Banos was sure to notice my car when he arrived to take over from Stanley Gertz, the old guy who handles my shift on my night off.

Even so, I could see who came and went from where I was, and had plenty of time to duck down under my dash when Cyril Parkus left at eight twenty and drove right past me.

I knew that Carol was right, but she just didn't get it. She wasn't immersed in the case the way I was. I couldn't go back to sitting in my shack, watching Cyril and Lauren Parkus come and go, without knowing the truth.

I didn't care whether it was my business or not.

And I was certain that most private eyes, at least most fictional ones, would agree with me on this, with the possible exception of Jim Rockford, who never did anything unless he was paid to or was forced into it at gunpoint.

So I sat there, waiting for something to happen.

As the hours passed, I found myself enjoying the wait, just sitting there watching the gate. There was something about being a private eye that gave even the simplest things in life more intensity. Even doing nothing suddenly had a thrilling edge to it.

It was certainly different from the experience of sitting in the shack and doing nothing.

I thought about going back to Swift Rent-A-Car and

trying to talk the lady behind the counter into giving me more on Arlo Pelz. I felt I handled myself well last time, and that maybe we connected in some way towards the end.

Then again, there might be something in the computer about what happened to Arlo's car, and if I walked in asking more questions, she might just call the cops on me.

I really had to find myself a big, brutal sidekick who wouldn't care about ethics, morality, or the law, and would be glad to do all the dangerous or tricky stuff that I didn't want to. I could send him to talk to her. He'd just walk in, stick his gun in the woman's face, and leave with a complete printout of the information I wanted.

I imagined him. A huge, bald, Asian guy with a dragon tattoo on his face. His name would be Drago. We'd engage in lots of witty, tough-guy repartee. We'd share a manly code of honor. He'd pick up my uniform at the dry cleaners'.

Around eleven, Lauren sped through the gate in her Range Rover. I started the car and really had to floor it to keep up with her, inadvertently letting a couple cars slip in between us. She was in a hurry to go somewhere, and I had a feeling it wasn't to get a cup of coffee.

I was excited. I had a hunch that my extra, added surveillance was going to have an immediate payoff. And then I was excited simply because I'd had a hunch. Before I became a private eye, I never had hunches.

Lauren raced down the hill towards the freeway. I wondered whether we'd be heading down to LA or up to Santa Barbara. I wondered if we'd be seeing Arlo Pelz again and if I'd have an opportunity to ambush him. When she passed the onramp, I knew we were going south.

But she suddenly came to a screeching stop in the middle of the freeway overpass, causing a domino-like chain reaction in the lane behind her. Everyone slammed on his brakes to avoid rear-ending the car in front of him. I was so busy trying not to become a Kia stain on the truck in front of me, I didn't even see Lauren get out of her car.

When I saw her again, she was already standing on the rail above the freeway.

She turned her head and looked right at me, her eyes blazing with the intensity of spotlights, exposing me and everything I ever thought or felt.

And then, before I could even blink, Lauren faced straight ahead and dove gracefully into the traffic below.

Chapter Eleven

◇ ◇ ◇

I never saw what happened next. But I heard it. The scraping and sliding and tearing and mashing of metal, glass, and flesh, and the moment afterward of unnatural stillness, when even time seemed shocked into immobility and silence, a stillness shattered by screams everywhere and the blur of people abandoning their cars, running down to the freeway to help the injured and the dead and to see the mess that one human being can make.

I backed up, made a screeching U-turn, and drove away. I didn't want to be any part of it.

But I already was.

Lauren told me as much with that look. She said: *I know you're there. I know what you've seen. Now watch this, asshole.*

Or maybe that wasn't what she said. Maybe she was asking me a question: *Why did you do this to me?*

I didn't know where to go or what to do. I just drove aimlessly. I wasn't aware of the traffic, of the stoplights, or even the car itself. I was fleeing.

All I saw was that horrible moment again and again, on an endless-replay loop in my mind. And the more I thought about it, the more frightened I became, the more my stomach churned and ached and seized up.

I finally stopped the car and puked in the street, my

broken ribs raging with pain with each deep, choking heave. When I was done, I leaned back against my car, clutching my sides, my whole body shaking, tears streaming down my checks.

And once again, I saw her head turning around slowly, her eyes intense, her lips curled in a tiny grimace.

She was looking *for me*. She wanted to be sure I was watching, that I would never forget.

And then Lauren was gone. Off the edge, taking me with her.

It was on the radio within the hour. I was somewhere out near Fillmore, driving aimlessly through the endless farmland, when I heard it.

They said a woman leaped to her death from a freeway overpass in Camarillo, causing a seventeen-car pile-up and injuring half a dozen people, two of them seriously.

Police had found her abandoned Range Rover and were withholding her identity until notification of next-of-kin.

Authorities said a full autopsy would be conducted to see if drugs or alcohol played a role in the horrific tragedy, but based on numerous witness accounts, they believed no foul play was involved.

They were calling it a suicide.

There was no mention of her looking at anybody first, or of the guy in the Kia Sephia who sped away from the scene.

No one was chasing me except my conscience, and that's how it would stay.

I knew that Cyril Parkus wouldn't tell them about her strange behavior, or that he'd hired a security guard to follow her around, or that somebody named Arlo Pelz was blackmailing her. I knew that despite the shock, the sorrow, and the disbelief, he would protect himself and her secret.

I had nothing to fear. And yet, I was terrified. Of what, I'm not sure. Maybe it was simply the knowledge that my presence alone could kill, that without even meeting someone, just by watching her, I could provoke death and injury.

That may have been why I was afraid, but it wasn't why I felt guilty.

I didn't really have a reason to be. I knew it wasn't my idea to follow her. I knew I wasn't the one blackmailing her and that I didn't push her off that overpass. I knew I had nothing to do with the secret that haunted her.

But I still felt guilty.

Because I was there.

Because she wanted me to.

Fillmore was a Hollywood-perfect recreation of a small town from the '30s, only with cars from the '90s filling the diagonal parking spaces.

Actually, the town had always looked like this, until it was decimated by the 1994 earthquake. They quickly rebuilt the Main Street, faithfully restoring everything to the way it had been.

But it wasn't really Fillmore any more, no matter how much they thought it was.

They had to know it, too; otherwise, why put historical placards on every building, detailing its history and rebirth?

It made the whole town feel like a museum exhibit. Because it was. An authentic recreation of a genuine California farming town.

Even so, walking down Main Street past the hardware store and pool hall and ice cream parlor was like stepping into an idealized, make-believe world, one more innocent and safe than the one we live in.

I don't know how I ended up there, but it was the perfect place for me to be. It didn't matter if Fillmore was real any more or not. In fact, it was probably better that it wasn't.

For the rest of the day, and into the night, I walked up and down the three blocks of Main Street, stopping to admire each and every window display. I sat in the park and fed the birds. I walked along the train tracks and had a slice of homemade pie at the diner.

I found a way to escape. I went to a place that didn't really exist. Where even the kids playing in the park looked like re-creations. I was half-tempted to see if they had historical placards around their necks.

I didn't think about Lauren Parkus.

I didn't think about myself.

I just went numb.

And then, when the clock tower above City Hall chimed at eleven p.m., I snapped out of it. It was time to return to the real world.

But I was going back a different man.

I became a re-creation of myself. I looked like Harvey Mapes once looked, but like Fillmore, something had been lost.

I got in my car and drove back through the orchards and up through the hills and down into Camarillo again.

I went to work.

I didn't know what else to do or where else to go. I just sat there and stared out into the night.

Around two a.m. the coyote showed up, stepping cautiously into the circle of light cast by the streetlamp. We looked at each other for a long moment, and then the telephone rang, startling us both.

The coyote ran away. I answered the phone.

"Front gate," I replied.

"I saw you this morning."

It was Cyril Parkus' voice.

It sounded like it was coming from the bottom of a deep, dark pit.

"You were parked on the side of the road," he said. "You tried to hide from me, but I knew you were there. Your windows were fogged up."

Maybe he should have been a detective. He could have saved me a lot of pain.

"If you knew," I asked, "why didn't you do something about it?"

There was a long silence. I didn't say anything, I just held the phone, listening to him breathe. His voice, when he finally spoke again, was almost a whisper.

"What did you see?"

"I saw her standing on the rail," I replied. "Lauren looked at me, and then she dove off as casually as if she were taking a swim."

"What did she want from you?"

"She wanted to make sure I was looking."

I was surprised by my own answer. It was simpler than the other explanations I'd run through my head. I wondered when I'd settled on this one.

"No, Harvey, she wanted to be sure that I was."

And then he hung up. I kept the phone to my ear.

I said, "Good night, Mr. Parkus." And then I hung up, too.

It took me fifteen minutes to walk up the steep hill to Cyril Parkus' house. I suppose a man in better shape would have made it in five, but I had to stop and rest a few times and clutch my sides in pain. I wasn't being a very good patient. I wasn't being much of a security guard, either.

I'd left the guard shack empty and the gate closed, but I knew from experience there was rarely anybody coming or going at two fifteen a.m. on a weeknight. I wasn't too worried.

We're also not supposed to enter the community, even though we guard it. Don't ask me why. So, to get in without ending up on the surveillance tape, I climbed over the gate at a spot where I know the camera's view is obstructed by an overgrown tree.

As I trudged up the steep hill, which would have been a chore for me even without the broken ribs, I tried to distract myself from the pain by looking at all the big houses I was theoretically protecting, with their detached garages and red-tile roofs and dramatic, outdoor lighting. It was as if the exterior of each house was decoratively pre-lit in case the cover photographer from *Architectural Digest* just happened to drive by, or maybe a busload of tourists, neither of which was likely to happen with the gate out front and my constant vigilance.

Well, almost constant.

All the lights were on inside and out at the Parkus house, and I heard the burbling of at least three different fountains as I walked across the cobblestones of the motor court.

The front door was almost entirely glass, so I could see straight through the circular, marble entry area into the huge, two-story living room, its floor-to-ceiling windows affording a commanding view of the entire valley.

But the view was lost on Cyril Parkus, who was sitting on the floor, staring blankly into the whiskey bottle between his legs. He was still dressed in his business suit, leaning against a wrought-iron and glass coffee table.

I knocked on the door. He looked over and didn't seem too surprised to see me.

He motioned me inside. I opened the door and went in. The house smelled like a rose garden, but there wasn't a single flower in sight.

"Come to check up on me?" Parkus asked.

"You didn't sound too good."

"Afraid I was gonna stick a gun in my mouth?"

I shrugged. There was alot of antique furniture and maritime oil paintings, but the room was dominated by an old, rotting, wooden sign above the fireplace. The faded, peeling paint read: Big Rock Lake Resort. It couldn't have been worth much, and didn't fit in with the rest of the décor, so I figured its value was sentimental.

"I could never do it, even though it's the Parkus family tradition." He shook his head and took a big swig from his bottle. "First my mom, then my sister, now my wife. All killed themselves. I must be a real horrible person to live with."

"You're not the reason she jumped."

Parkus cocked his head. "Really? And how the fuck would you know that? You've never even talked to her."

"I saw her face when she met Arlo Pelz," I said. "I bet if he'd never shown up, she'd still be alive."

"We'll never know, will we?"

"We could try."

"Un-fucking-believable." He glared at me, set his bottle down on the floor, and struggled to his feet. "Is that what you came here for, Harvey, to shake me down for a few more bucks?"

Parkus reached into his pocket, pulled out his money-clip, and threw the cash at me.

"Go ahead," he yelled, "take it!"

"I want to earn it, Mr. Parkus. I want to bring Arlo Pelz to justice."

"Jesus Christ," he snorted in disbelief. "I hired you do to something anybody with a driver's license and a two-digit IQ could pull off, and now you think you're fucking Batman."

"Arlo Pelz might as well have pushed your wife off that overpass," I said. "And you're going to let him just walk away. Well, maybe you can, but I can't."

It was true. At that moment, I felt like I was channeling Joe Mannix, Frank Cannon, Barnaby Jones, Thomas Magnum, and all the great private eyes who came before me. Even Parkus seemed to sense that.

"Who the fuck are you?" Parkus yelled, his voice echoing off the walls of his big, wide living room. "You're not a police officer, you're not even a security guard. You're barely even a man. You're just a clown with an iron-on badge."

He looked so disgusted at the sight of me, I thought he might vomit right there. But I felt stronger and more sure of myself than I ever had in my life.

Parkus marched over to the front door and held it open.

"Get out of my house, Harvey. Go back down to your little shack and pick your nose for a few more hours. And if you ever butt into my life again, if you so much as wave to me as I drive by, I'll have you fired. Do we understand each other?"

I understood, all right.

The only reason he wasn't going to have me fired the next day was because he was still afraid of what I knew, or might know, or could figure out. He couldn't take the risk that I might go to the police with my story.

I walked out.

"I'm sorry for your loss," I said as I left.

He slammed the door behind me.

I was glad I came up. I'd learned a lot and, without even realizing it, made some decisions.

In a way, Arlo Pelz and I now had something in common. We both had something on Cyril Parkus. Arlo had Lauren's secret, whatever it was, and I knew that she was being blackmailed, and that her husband knew the guy who was doing it.

It didn't seem like I had all that much, but it was enough to make Cyril Parkus very nervous. Enough to try buying me off and, when that failed, using intimidation to get his way.

Neither worked. If anything, he'd encouraged me.

I was going to find Arlo Pelz and whatever it was that Lauren killed herself to escape.

The only trouble was, I had no idea how I was going to do it.

Chapter Twelve

$$\diamondsuit \quad \diamondsuit \quad \diamondsuit$$

Carol was waiting for me at the Caribbean, sitting on a chaise lounge facing the entrance. She was in her business clothes, and she had the morning paper on the chaise lounge next to her.

"Shouldn't you be on your way to work?" I asked.

"I thought you'd want to talk."

"About what?"

She held up the Valley section of the *Los Angeles Times*. On the front page was a picture of Lauren, which I guessed was taken at a party, a picture of the wrecked cars on the freeway, and an article about the suicide.

I took the paper and quickly scanned the article. It was mostly about the traffic accident she caused, and the people in the hospital, who were in satisfactory condition with all kinds of broken bones. There was a little bit about Lauren and how shocked the community was by her suicide. The article said she was an active fundraiser for local charities and was survived by her husband in Camarillo and a mother in Seattle.

I handed the paper back to Carol. "I told you she needed help."

Carol nodded. "I'm sorry, Harvey."

"It's not your fault." I was saying that a lot lately.

"It's not yours, either."

I nodded, but really only to be polite. I wasn't sure she was right. I told her that I saw the suicide, and that I'd talked to Cyril Parkus, and that even though he threatened me, I was going to continue my investigation.

Carol smiled, which I thought was kind of odd.

"I knew you would," she said, like she was glad, or proud of me, when just the other night she was scowling with disapproval over the idea that I hadn't walked away from it. I'll never understand women.

"I think I can help you," she said. "Do you still have that car rental agreement?"

"Yeah, why?"

"I'd like to take it to work with me; maybe I can use Arlo's Visa card number to run a credit check on him and get you an address."

That was a great idea.

Who'd have thought having a friend at a mortgage company would come in handy on an investigation?

I was learning that there were other ways for a private eye to get information without having a love-hate relationship with a cop.

"You're my Peggy *and* my Susan Silverman," I said.

"Who are they?" she asked.

"Peggy was the secretary for private eye Joe Mannix. She did all the important research for him while he ran around beating people up. Susan Silverman is a shrink who sleeps with Spenser, another private eye. She gives him philosophical insight into how noble and good he is and they are, and how it's okay he's killed a dozen people because he's so noble and good, and then she fucks his brains out."

"Is this your way of saying you expect me to go to bed with you now?"

That hadn't occurred to me, but since she'd mentioned it, I didn't want to entirely dismiss the idea.

"No, but if that's what you want . . ." I let my voice trail off suggestively.

"Get me the rental agreement, Harvey."

She said it in a way that not only made it clear my suggestion was rejected, but that she was disappointed with me again. Somehow, that made me feel a lot more at ease with her.

I got up. "Can I use your computer while you're at work?"

She tossed me the keys to her place. "Make yourself at home."

I started for my apartment, then turned back to look at her and caught her looking at me. The expression on her face wasn't the lingering traces of disappointment I'd expected. I saw warmth and concern and even some sadness.

"Why do you want to help me?" I asked.

"I've never seen you care about something before," she said. The answer came so easily for her, I wondered if she'd been waiting for the question.

"I care about you," I replied.

"It's different now," she said.

I supposed it was, but I didn't want to get into it then. I didn't know if I *ever* wanted to. I nodded in what I hoped was a deep, introspective way, and went to get her the rental agreement. I felt her eyes on me the whole way, but this time I didn't look back.

Carol's apartment had the same floor plan as mine, but that's where the similarities ended. It was decorated like some kind of frilly country cottage, with yellow walls, white trim, and everything she could afford from the Restoration Hardware and Pottery Barn catalogs.

She'd replaced all the door knobs and drawer handles and faucet fixtures with replicas of old-fashioned stuff, and every surface in her place had some kind of cutesy accessory, whether it was the colorful oven-mitts on the kitchen counter, the napkins in their special holder on the table, or the seatcovers on all the chairs.

There were also plug-in air fresheners in every electrical outlet, which made the whole apartment smell so strongly of pine sap, I felt like I was visiting an upscale tree house.

Ordinarily, I felt uncomfortable in her apartment and fled as soon as possible. But this time, I was concentrating so much on her computer screen, I was oblivious to my environment.

First, I used a search engine to see what I could find on the Internet about Lauren Parkus. I found lots of articles, mostly local society columns, about parties and fundraisers she either organized or had attended. The events were always very pricey affairs for good causes at five-star hotels, and the guest lists usually included some movie stars, major sports figures, and big corporate leaders.

There were also a few pictures of her. Each time one came up on screen, it startled me. Her eyes always looked so alive. Of course, nothing about her was alive any more.

Cyril Parkus was often in the photographs with his wife, a big, proud smile on his face. He seemed so glad to be there, as if he was having such a good time battling cancer, illiteracy, lupus, sudden infant death syndrome, teenage drug addiction, and pollution of our groundwater. They were just parties to him—I think they were more to Lauren, or at least I wanted to believe they were. He also held her in a possessive kind of way that declared, *I get to take her home and fuck her and you don't.*

I looked up Cyril Parkus. There were even more articles

about him than his wife, mostly business pieces about the financial side of the movies. Apparently he was a major player in the international sale and distribution of movies. Anytime there was an article about the field, he was the expert they quoted. I guess he qualified as an "industry leader." I figured it was his stature in the business that got so many people to contribute and participate in the charities Lauren was involved in.

Just for the hell of it, I tried looking up Arlo Pelz in a few of those Internet phone book and "find your lost friend, lover, or relative" websites, but came up empty. I also ran my name on those same sites, and wasn't surprised that nothing turned up for me, either. We were both as irrelevant in cyberspace as we were in the real world.

But I was going to find him, somehow, and I was going to make him pay for blackmailing Lauren Parkus and driving her to commit suicide. I also intended to get him back for kicking the piss out of me.

Intention and ability are two very different things.

I wasn't a martial artist or a boxer. I had no self-defense skills at all, unless you include running and hiding. The last actual fistfight I'd been in was in the fourth grade and it went a lot like that fight in the elevator, with the other guy doing all the hitting and kicking and me doing all the crying.

I didn't have time to find a master of the ancient art of Sinanju and learn how to turn a napkin into a lethal weapon.

If I wanted to take Arlo, it couldn't be a fair fight. I needed an edge.

With that in mind, the next thing I did was go back to the search engine and type in the phrases: " 'Realistic toy gun' AND 'police shooting.' " The search engine coughed up a couple hundred articles about police officers shooting kids and morons who pointed fake guns at them. I scanned the articles and narrowed my search until I found the brand name and model of a toy gun that did the best job of fooling the police and getting kids and morons killed.

It was an exact, plastic replica of a Desert Eagle semi-automatic pistol that fired BBs. I found the manufacturer's website and learned they also made detailed replicas of just about every other pistol, machine gun, and rifle you could imagine.

The air-fired BB guns were intended mostly for target shooting, but were also used a lot in movie and TV production as stand-ins for the real thing. By law, the replica guns came with a bright orange tip on the barrel so they couldn't be mistaken for genuine firearms. But it wasn't hard to break the tip off, or paint it, and trick someone holding a real weapon into shooting you five or six times.

The fake Desert Eagle semi-automatic pistol sold for about forty bucks, a fraction of the cost of a real one, and required no license or waiting period. All you had to be was over twenty-one years old and gun crazy.

That's when Carol called, excitement in her voice. She'd discovered that the credit card Arlo Pelz used was shared with his wife, Jolene, that the card was officially in her name, and that the bills were sent to her in Snohomish, Washington, which was just outside Seattle.

I got a chill up my back, just like the one I got when Bruce Willis saw the wedding ring drop out of his wife's hand in *The Sixth Sense.*

I checked the article about Lauren Parkus' suicide again, to be sure the chill I felt wasn't lightheadedness from inhaling all that pine air freshener. It wasn't. The article said Lauren's mother lived in Seattle.

I got the chill again and told Carol why. I think I heard her swallow a squeal. It was kind of like we were having phone sex, saying the things we knew would get the other person off.

"If anybody finds out what I was doing, I could get fired for this, but I don't care," Carol admitted, her hushed voice tittering with excitement. "It was fun."

She'd discovered my awful secret. Snooping was a thrill, so much so that she'd easily forgotten the dark side, the whole reason she was looking into Arlo Pelz for me: *somebody died.* I didn't have the heart to remind her. Carol did me a favor; she deserved to enjoy it.

"You have something else I can do?" she whispered conspiratorially.

I told her there wasn't and thanked her for what she'd found out. I also told her I wouldn't be around when she got back and that I'd leave her keys in my mailbox.

Then I called my supervisor at the security company, told him I had a horrible stomach flu, and that I'd probably be out for a couple days.

And then I printed out the specs on the Desert Eagle and a list of the manufacturer's retailers in Seattle.

When I got to LAX, I discovered that the airline had overbooked my flight. They were offering four hundred dollars in free travel vouchers to any volunteers who were willing to give up their seats and wait for the next flight to Seattle in three hours.

I wasn't in a hurry. Lauren Parkus was already dead. Three hours wouldn't change much. I volunteered my narrow coach seat and five inches of legroom.

I got my free travel voucher and, feeling flush, went to the restaurant and treated myself to one of their eight-dollar-

and-ninety-five-cent cheeseburgers and two-fifty Cokes.

It was only while I was sitting there, eating my insanely expensive fast food, that I started thinking about things. First, I wondered how the public allowed airports and movie theatres to charge so goddamn much for food. Then I thought about what I'd do when I got to Seattle.

I hadn't made any concrete, or even sketchy, plans yet. I'd been so caught up in the excitement of my discoveries, I'd just let the momentum carry me along.

The only thing I knew for sure was that I was going to the Snohomish address where the credit card bills were sent, but I didn't know what I was going to do when I got there, how I'd capture Arlo, and what I'd do with him once I did.

I wondered what the Seattle connection was, and if maybe Arlo or his wife Jolene were relatives of Lauren's. I also wondered what kind of woman would marry Arlo Pelz and if she was involved with the blackmail scheme, too. And if she was, what was I going to do about her? What if neither one of them was there? What would I do then?

I could go and talk to Lauren's mother, for one thing. Maybe she could tell me something about Arlo or Jolene or Lauren that would help me figure everything out.

And that's when I realized there was something else I didn't know: Lauren's maiden name.

How was I supposed to find her mother without knowing at least that?

It was a good thing I volunteered to sit the flight out, because I wouldn't have discovered until much later how ill-prepared I was for the journey.

So I sat there in the criminally overpriced airport restaurant, nursing my Coke and thinking hard, hoping the slow trickle of sugar and caffeine into my system would jump-start my brain.

I started by asking myself who would know the name of Lauren's mother. Cyril Parkus certainly would, but I couldn't ask him. The police probably knew, but I wasn't brave enough to call them. I was fucked.

If only the *LA Times* reporter had asked for Lauren's maiden name when he was writing his story, he could have saved me a lot of trouble.

Thinking about the *LA Times* made me think about what I read on the can in the guard shack. I mean, what I read besides the paperbacks and the two-year-old copy of a *Sports Illustrated* swimsuit edition.

I found a pay phone, called the *Camarillo Star-News*, and asked for the city desk. I told the editor I was from The AIDS Crack Baby Rescue Alliance, and that we wanted to send a wreath to Lauren Parkus' mother, in honor of all the money her daughter had raised to help crack babies with AIDS, and asked if he had a name or address for her. I even started sobbing to drive home my sorrow and genuine desperation.

He gave me the name, Mona Harper, and told me that she lived in Seattle, and that was all he knew. He did ask me why it sounded like I was calling from an airport. I sobbed some more and told him I was on my way to South America, to help all the malnourished, crack babies with AIDS down there. He was so touched, he wanted to make a donation to the A.C.B.R.A. in Lauren's name. I made up a post office box address and tearfully hung up.

There's a good reason why an editor ends up at the *Camarillo Star-News* instead of the *LA Times*, and that's why I called him.

I wiped my eyes and went to the newsstand, where I bought a couple Sue Grafton and Robert Crais mysteries. I found a seat and started reading right away. I couldn't help feeling like I was cramming before my final exams.

Chapter Thirteen

◇ ◇ ◇

By the time the plane landed at the Seattle-Tacoma International Airport early that evening, I'd finished the Grafton book and was almost finished with the Crais. I can't say I consciously learned anything from the exploits of Kinsey Milhone and Elvis Cole, but I hoped something had sunk in by osmosis.

On my way through the terminal, I stopped at a gift shop and bought some Pepto-Bismol and Advils which, in my haste to get going, I'd forgotten to pack. Between the uncomfortable coach seat and my anxiety, my accumulated injuries were flaring up badly.

I washed down five or six Advils with a mouthful of Pepto-Bismol, then hobbled over to the Swift Rent-A-Car counter, which was located in the parking structure outside, across from the terminal.

I'd never been to Seattle before, and I didn't know what kind of trouble I might get into or how far I might have to travel in the course of my investigation. So, I decided to step up from my Kia into something a bit more aggressive. The best they had to offer was a Buick LeSabre Custom. I took it and was careful to choose every insurance option they offered.

The LeSabre was the size of my apartment. The simu-

lated wood-grain interior trim and the decoratively pat-
terned cloth seats gave me a flashback to my mom's
Oldsmobile Cutlass station wagon and the fights my sister
and I used to have over who got to sit "in the way-back."
When my mother abandoned us, she gladly left the Cutlass
station wagon behind. My father lost it a few months later
to pay gambling debts, but we really didn't miss it.

Anyway, the LeSabre, with its big bench seats, would be
comfortable to sleep in if I had to. The engine had some
guts, and the power steering was so loose, if I broke every
finger except one, I'd still be able to turn the wheel.

That was good to know.

I didn't have to drive far from Sea-Tac before I came
upon a Borders bookstore off the freeway. I didn't realize
then that the only thing that outnumbered bookstores in Seattle were coffee houses or I might have kept on driving. Instead, I stopped there and bought an illustrated city guide
and a detailed map book of Seattle-area streets.

I went back to my LeSabre, took out my list of retailers
selling those replica Desert Eagle guns, and looked for the
nearest store. I got lucky; there was one a few blocks away.
It was called The Northwest Sportsman.

The sportsman at the counter was shaped like a Her-
shey's Kiss and had one more chin than was absolutely necessary. He wanted to impress me with his encyclopedic
knowledge of BB guns, which I was sure was only rivaled by
his knowledge of comic books.

The sportsman held the plastic gun loosely in his hand
and grinned at it in admiration as he spoke.

"This here is a spring-loaded, single-shot, low-volume
air pistol. The real Desert Eagle is manufactured in Israel,
but this baby comes to us straight from Tokyo. The styling
is nearly indistinguishable from the genuine article," he

said, drawling out the pronunciation of those last two words so they came out as *genu-wine art-eekle.*

"The body is ABS plastic, the internal parts are metal," he went on. "It's got a 113-millimeter barrel and a muzzle velocity of two hundred thirty-five feet per second, firing .2-gram plastic BBs. But the beauty of this piece is the subtle tonal differences in the molding and coloring that—"

I interrupted him.

"I just want to shoot some bottles and look cool doing it," I said. "I don't need to know all the details."

For a minute, I thought he was so offended that he wouldn't sell it to me, but his commercial instincts easily overcame his personal pride and he finally forked the weapon over. He didn't say a single word after that.

I bought a belt-clip holster to go with the gun and some BBs, so I'd appear to be a genu-wine enthusiast. The bill came to nearly a hundred bucks. I saved the receipt for my taxes.

On the way out, I spotted a hardware store across the street. I stowed my gun in the trunk, went to the store, and bought a roll of duct tape, a sledgehammer, and a can of black spray paint. I saved that receipt, too.

I was ready for action.

Once inside my two-star hotel room a few blocks away, I laid out some newspaper in the bathtub and spray-painted over the bright orange tip of the gun, adding my own subtle, tonal differences to the molding and coloring. I left the gun in the tub to dry.

I could hear the planes rumbling overhead, but it didn't bother me much. It reminded me how much I was saving on accommodations and made me feel responsible. There's no reason to spend more than thirty bucks a night for a mattress, a toilet, and a sink, especially for a hardened, professional private eye on assignment.

I sat down at the table, spread the map out in front of me, and located the address near Snohomish where Arlo Pelz lived. I put an X on the spot; then I took out a pen and traced the best route there. It was a small town on the Snohomish River in Snohomish County, about forty miles northeast of Seattle.

I also looked up Mona Harper's address in the phone book, found it on the map, and put an X there, too. She lived in a Seattle neighborhood called Madison Park, on the shore of Lake Washington, near one of the city's floating bridges. It sounded like a term a spokesman for the bridge might use to spin things after a disaster. "The bridge hasn't really collapsed," he'd say, "it's just floating."

I always thought bridges were supposed to go over the water, but what did I know? Up here, they probably called those flying bridges or something.

Now that I'd mastered the terrain, and had a vague idea of what I intended to do, I called Carol and told her my plan. I told her if she didn't hear from me at the same time tomorrow, to call the Seattle police.

"And tell them what, exactly?" she asked.

"Tell them I'm dead," I replied.

"That's not going to do you much good."

"Okay, so tell them I'm probably dead," I said, "or I will be if they don't rescue me."

"You think the police will care?"

I was in uncharted territory here, since most private eyes I knew about never told anyone where they were going or what they were doing. But they were braver than me, and certainly never pissed themselves in a fistfight.

"If I had a friend on the force, they would," I said.

"Getting myself one is at the top of my list of things to do, if I don't get killed and decide to continue in this field."

"Don't do anything stupid, Harvey."

It was probably way too late for that advice. "I never intend to," I said.

There was an uncomfortable silence on the phone.

"Come back soon," she said.

"I'll call you tomorrow."

I hung up and thought about all the implications of her last words. Then I wondered if it would be against the private eye code of conduct to watch a double feature of *The Horny Contortionist* and *Where The Boys Aren't* on pay-per-view.

I decided it wouldn't be and reached for the remote.

I didn't sleep much. Part of the problem with working nights is that your biological clock, or whatever the hell they call it, gets all out of whack. Having a couple broken ribs didn't help. So I only got a couple hours' worth of sleep, mostly catnaps during the slow parts of the porn movies. I also slept a little bit sitting on the toilet, where I discovered the consequences of amateur pharmacology.

I was ready to check out and get going as soon as the sun came up, what little of it I could see through the gray, cloudy skies. I put on a jacket and tie and by seven a.m. I was on Interstate 5, heading towards downtown Seattle.

I was struck by a couple things right away. The crisp, clean air to start with. My sinuses weren't used to that, so I kept sneezing and my nose was running. If you can't taste the air when you breathe it, it's too clean.

Next thing I noticed was the drizzle. I seemed to be the only guy on the road with his windshield wipers on, so I guessed it was like this all the time and that people there were so used to it, they'd learned to see through the layer of water on the glass.

Finally, there was the green. There was so much vegetation everywhere, even along the freeway, it made LA seem like nothing but concrete and asphalt, which I suppose it was.

As the freeway cut through downtown, I craned my neck like a tourist to get a few good looks at the Space Needle. It was actually the least impressive of the tall buildings that made up the skyline, but at least I was certain I was in Seattle.

The farther out of the city I got, the greener the landscape became. Just before reaching Everett, I took the turn-off for Highway 96. Things became what I'd call rural after that, the narrow highway passing through hilly forests, and lots of mailboxes on posts in front of dirt roads that led who-knows-where. Around the intersection with Highway 9, just outside Snohomish, there were a couple motels facing each other on either side of the road. I made a mental note of them and continued on towards town.

Snohomish wasn't really a town anymore, it was more of a theme for a shopping center. The quaint, nineteenth-century buildings at the heart of the old logging town were almost all occupied by antique stores and indoor swap-meets. That's what they do with dead towns now, they turn them into antique malls.

I drove through town and into the country again, past lots of rusted-out cars, rundown farms, and old, rotting houses until I came to a batch of mailboxes at a turn-off for a long, dirt road.

I drove up the muddy road, lined on both sides with tall weeds, and took a fork that was marked by a weatherbeaten wood sign that'd been spray-painted with Pelz's address.

I thought about stopping, and walking the rest of the way in, to be more stealthy, but figured I'd get bogged down in the mud. Besides, if things went bad, I didn't want to be too far from my car and a quick escape. I decided to take my chances with a direct approach and I drove on.

The road curved and suddenly spilled out into a clearing. There was a faded mobile home, a ten-year-old, corroded Chevy Lumina parked beside it. A clothesline was loosely strung between two trees. There was a barbecue, a picnic table, a couple of lawn chairs in search of a lawn, and an old couch sinking in the mud. The stripped, sheet-metal carcasses of a few decaying cars were scattered amidst the weeds on the edges of the clearing. It all fit with my initial impression of Arlo Pelz.

I parked beside the Lumina and sat a minute, my heart racing. I don't know which I felt more, terror or excitement, but I knew I couldn't just sit there. I blew my nose into a napkin and tossed it on the floor. I took my toy gun out of the glove box, leaned forward, and slipped it into the holster that was clipped to my belt behind my back, underneath my jacket. That was the way Mannix used to do it.

I eased out of the car and approached the door, one hand behind my back, ready to whip out my gun if Arlo gave me trouble. I'd lead him to my car, tie his wrists up with duct tape, and then make him think I was going to execute him unless he talked. Once he told me everything, and wet his pants, I'd take him in. The wetting-his-pants part was real important to me.

The key to my plan was the assumption that Arlo would be unarmed. That didn't seem like a big assumption until I approached the mobile home.

What if he burst out right now with a sawed-off shotgun

in his hands? Did I really believe I could hold him off with my state-of-the-art BB gun?

I was about to go back to my car and drive away until I could come up with a better plan, when the door opened and Jolene Pelz stepped out in a pink bathrobe, wrapped tight around what I presumed was her naked body, looking tired and pissed-off.

"Who the hell are you and what are you doing here so God-damn early in the morning?" she said.

Jolene Pelz had the basic framework for beauty, a nice body and attractive face, but her attributes were eroded by a lifetime of bitter disappointment, which she wore on her skin, carried on her back, and expressed with a weariness that marbled her voice. No amount of make-up, perfume, jewelry, or designer clothing would ever hide it, not that she was even trying.

"I'm looking for Arlo Pelz," I said.

"He isn't here. In fact, he doesn't live here anymore."

"That's not what it says on his credit card bills, Mrs. Pelz."

"What kind of cop are you?"

I was so flattered that I almost smiled. I actually radiated copliness now. Wow. That had to say something fundamental about how much I'd changed, about the self-confidence I now radiated, even if I didn't feel it.

"Credit card," I said. "My name is Frank Furillo. I'm a fraud investigator for Visa."

She leaned against her door. "The cop on *Hill Street Blues* was named Furillo."

If I was going to continue in this business, I had to stop assuming I was the only guy who watched TV and read books.

"I know," I said wearily. "But it's not so bad. I grew up

with a kid named James Bond. He got his ass kicked every day of the week."

"Probably by a guy like Arlo," she said. "You want some coffee?"

"That would be nice."

"All I got is instant," she said and went back inside.

I took my hand off my toy gun and followed her in.

Chapter Fourteen

The place was laid out a lot like Jim Rockford's mobile home, only where his desk would be there was a tan, pseudo-suede couch, the kind that had bulging cushions when you bought it but that flattened to the width of typing paper within a month after you got it home. The cushions were still plump.

That caught my eye, and so did the big-screen TV that dominated the boxy living room.

Jolene asked me to sit down on the couch while she made the coffee, but I couldn't. I was afraid my clip-on holster would come off and that, with my broken ribs, I'd have a hard time getting up again after I sunk into the cushions.

So I stood at the low, chipped Formica counter that separated the kitchen area from the living room and watched her set the water to boil. There were bills, magazines, and a high school yearbook cluttering the countertop. I resisted the urge to rummage through them.

Jolene washed out two coffee mugs and dried them off.

"What's this about?" she asked.

This was my first time questioning somebody, and my second attempt at subterfuge, and I didn't want to blow it. I reminded myself that when she first saw me, she thought I was a cop. Everything I said and did now had to reinforce that first impression. I couldn't show any doubt or hesitation. I couldn't let my nose run and I couldn't sniffle.

"We noticed an unusual flurry of activity on your account in a very short period of time," I said. "Were you aware that your husband stayed at the Universal Sheraton in Los Angeles last week and ran up a bill of twelve hundred and fifteen dollars?"

"No," she cinched the robe even tighter around herself. I looked past her to the open door of the bedroom. I could see one corner of an unmade bed and a pair of tennis shoes on the floor. I'd seen them before, coming at my face.

"Did you know he rented a Ford Focus from Swift Rent-A-Car, which he returned after a week with two thousand three hundred and eighty-seven dollars in uninsured body damage?"

"I don't know anything about that."

"His name is on the account, which makes you responsible for his charges and the damage to the vehicle."

I glanced at the yearbook on the counter. On the cover it read: Marcus Whitman High School, 1986.

"It's a mistake," Jolene said, cinching her robe again, even though it hadn't loosened up any in the last twenty seconds. "I put his name on the account when we got married and I forgot it was there, or I would have taken it off when he went to prison. I certainly would have taken it off after the divorce."

This was getting interesting. I decided to give her a little something to hang some hope on as a reward. "It's true that we haven't seen his signature on a credit slip in quite some time."

"Four years."

"That was one of the things that seemed suspicious to us," I said. "Still, the fact remains he is an authorized user.

Technically, the charges are valid."

I didn't want to give her too much hope. I wanted her to have a reason to answer my questions, to try to convince me to write off the mythical thirty five hundred dollars.

"You have to believe me, I didn't remember he was on the card," she whined. "We're divorced; why the hell would I pay his bills anymore?"

"When did you divorce him?"

"Right after he went to prison," she said.

"What did he go to prison for?"

"He was a drug dealer," she said. "Not a very good one. He used too much of what he sold. So did I."

It was a nice try, that little bit of self-recrimination, but she wasn't getting any sympathy from me. "When was he released?"

"About six months ago."

The teapot whistled. She poured the water into the mugs.

"You're not gonna make me pay for all that stuff, are you?" she asked. "I mean, doesn't the fact that we're legally divorced make what *he* did fraud? I mean, doesn't that make you and me the victims?"

"How did he get the card?" I asked.

Jolene dropped a couple spoonfuls of coffee crystals into the cups and stirred them while she thought about her answer.

"All his mail was forwarded to him in prison," she said tentatively. "I guess that included credit cards."

That didn't make much sense to me. I couldn't see prison officials letting inmates receive credit cards in the mail. Couldn't the cards be sharpened into shivs or something? But I had to give her points for thinking fast on her feet. I decided to make my next move while she was still off-balance. I headed for the bedroom like I paid the mortgage.

"What are you doing?" she asked, dropping the spoon with a clank into the sink.

I strode directly into the bedroom before I replied. "Looking for the bathroom."

The closet doors were open, so Arlo wasn't hiding in there. Her panties and bra were on the floor. She'd taken them off in a hurry. The bed didn't have a mattress frame; the box spring was right on the floor. There was no way he could be hiding under the bed.

"The bathroom is over here," she said from behind me.

I turned around and she knocked on the door that was between the kitchen and the bedroom.

"Thanks," I said.

She opened it. The bathroom was empty. I went inside and closed the door behind me. It reminded me of an airplane lavatory, only not as roomy. I looked at myself in the mirror and pondered my next move.

The first thing I did was take some toilet paper and blow my nose, which hurt my ribs, and I was reminded again of how they were broken.

Those were definitely Arlo's tennis shoes in the bedroom. He'd been here, maybe only moments ago. They'd probably heard my car coming up the road long before I got there.

If Arlo was still around, he was outside hiding somewhere, shivering in the wet weeds. Maybe he was waiting to ambush me, but I doubted it.

I flushed the toilet, washed my hands, and came out again. My coffee was waiting for me on the counter, an issue of *Cosmo* serving as a coaster.

Jolene sipped her coffee and looked at me over the rim of the mug.

"When was the last time you saw your ex-husband?" I asked.

"March twenty-seventh," she blurted out.

That was roughly three weeks ago, about the time Lauren started acting funny. "How can you be so sure of the date?"

"It was the day after my high school reunion," she held up her yearbook. "I was a cheerleader."

"Really?"

Jolene opened the book and proudly showed me the picture. It was taken of her in mid-leap, pom-poms in the air, a big smile on her face. She was pure beauty then, unblemished by the disappointments that burdened her now. She stared at the photo as if it were a diamond.

"You were very pretty," I said.

"Yes, I was." She abruptly closed the book.

"What was Arlo doing here?" I asked.

"He wanted to borrow some money. I told him to get fucked," she replied, studying me now. "You ask an awful lot of personal questions for a guy checking on some credit card purchases."

"It's my job to determine whether we swallow the charges or you do, and I have to support my decision with the circumstances surrounding the transactions," I said, realizing I'd let her put me momentarily on the defensive. That had to be corrected. I looked over at the big-screen TV and the puffy couch. "I don't recall seeing those on your statement."

"They were a gift," she said quickly. "From my aunt."

"Lucky you," I said dryly. I pulled a photo of Lauren Parkus from my jacket pocket. It was one of the special ones I'd taken for myself. "Do you know this woman?"

She gave the picture a quick glance. "Was she using my credit card, too?"

I just looked at her. She sighed and looked at the picture again. I studied her face to see if I could detect a reaction. What I saw was a woman afraid of being stuck with a thirty-five-hundred-dollar bill. I didn't see anything else.

"Who is she?" Jolene asked.

"Her name is Lauren Parkus," I said, looking again for a reaction and not getting one. "We suspect your ex-husband was seeing her in LA, that she might be involved."

When I said that, Jolene sighed with relief. "So, you're not going to make me pay. You believe me."

I pocketed the photo. "I've still got to verify what you've told me. But if it checks out, we'll pursue Mr. Pelz for the money. If we decide to press charges, you may be hearing from the FBI."

"The FBI?"

"He crossed state lines in the commission of a felony," I said. "That makes it a Federal offense."

I didn't know what the hell I was talking about. I was making it up as I went along. But I wanted to scare her. Then I remembered something I read in a detective novel once, I couldn't remember which one, but it confirmed my faith in learning-by-osmosis.

"I'll be staying at the Sno-Inn for the night," I said, referring to one of the two motels I saw on opposite sides of the highway as I drove in. "If you think of anything that might help me locate Arlo, give me a call."

I headed for the door, opening it slowly, my hand behind my back near my gun, in case Arlo was waiting on the other side to clobber me.

He wasn't.

I relaxed and walked out. She stood in the doorway and

watched me go to my car.

"The Sno-Inn Motel is a dump," she said.

I smiled at her. "I'm frugal."

I got in the car, made a wide U-turn, and drove off. I checked my rearview mirror for a glimpse of Arlo as I left the clearing, but if he was there, he didn't come out of hiding.

Overall, I was pleased with my performance. I learned a lot of useful information. In my estimation, I was getting pretty slick.

I would have liked to stake the place out, but I didn't see a way to pull it off. I wasn't about to park the car and creep back up there. If he was there, he'd be expecting that, so that would be stupid. And if he decided to flee in the Lumina, I'd be stuck up there on foot. And if he wasn't around now, there was no place to stash the car and still keep my eye on the dirt road without him spotting me when he came back. I just didn't see a way to go after him for the moment that didn't put me at a big disadvantage.

But I wasn't concerned. I had a feeling I wouldn't have to go after him. I had a feeling he'd come after me.

Chapter Fifteen

$$\diamond \quad \diamond \quad \diamond$$

On my way back to Seattle to see Mona Harper, Lauren's mother, I took an hour out to do a little sightseeing. I did it to reward myself and work up the courage to talk with her.

I stopped in Pioneer Square because that's what my guidebook recommended. It also recommended I take the tour of underground Seattle, but I figured if they decided to bury it, nobody thought it was much to look at to begin with.

So I parked on a side street near the cobblestone plaza and walked around the neighborhood, seeking shelter from the drizzle under a Victorian-looking, iron-and-glass pergola.

I studied the passers-by and thought about what I'd learned from my visit with Jolene. I learned that cheerleaders may have it great in high school, but that things evened out later. And I learned that Arlo Pelz used to be a drug dealer and served time in prison, so blackmail wasn't a big moral dilemma for him.

He'd definitely seen his ex-wife since he'd returned from Los Angeles. I knew that from the tennis shoes by the bed. And I was pretty certain the new TV and couch were bought with the piss-soaked blackmail money. What I didn't know was whether Jolene knew that's where his money came from. I was sure she gave Arlo the credit card, but she might not have known about the trip to LA or anything about Lauren Parkus.

But now they both knew I was on the case and, judging by Arlo's reaction to me in Santa Monica, I knew he wouldn't be too happy about the news, especially if he caught a peek at me and recognized me from the elevator. I figured he might do something rash and save me the trouble of cooking up some way to sneak up on him.

I'd be able to get more out of Arlo if I could make him think I knew more than I actually did. Private eyes pulled that trick all the time.

I didn't come to any new conclusions about the case while I was standing there, but I discovered I could tell the tourists from the locals pretty easily. The tourists were the ones hiding from the drizzle under umbrellas. The locals were the ones who only needed a lid for their espressos.

Just about everybody, except the obvious tourists, seemed to have a cup of coffee in one hand and a novel in the other. Apparently, there was a city ordinance that required everybody to join Oprah's book club and declare a favorite coffee blend. Even the bums were sipping Starbucks and reading Barbara Kingsolver.

So, before going back to the car, I stopped at the Elliot Bay Bookstore, bought an Anita Shreve novel, and snagged an empty Starbucks cup from the trash can outside, in case I ever needed to blend in with the crowd.

I drove east on Madison Street until it ended at the lake and a little shopping village that seemed to cater to well-heeled retirees and rich, young couples.

There was a small park and beach, but otherwise the shore was lined with apartment buildings that jutted out on pilings into the cold, emerald water. I wondered what would happen to the buildings in an earthquake. Californians can't help but wonder about that.

Mrs. Harper's apartment building was the tallest, at about ten stories, and the apartments on the end had big decks that commanded unobstructed views of the floating bridge and snow-capped Mount Rainier in the distance.

I parked the car in front of her building, walked up to the lobby, and found her name on the directory by the locked front door. I punched in the number of her unit on the security keypad and rang her up.

"Yes?" her voice crackled with static. There were Jack-in-the-Box drive-thrus with better speaker systems.

"Mrs. Harper?" I replied.

"Yes?"

"My name is Harvey Mapes, I'm a detective with Westland Security. Your son-in-law, Cyril Parkus, hired me to investigate your daughter's death."

I waited for her to say something, but the speaker just hissed.

"I'd like to come up and ask you a few questions."

"Cyril didn't say anything to me about this," she said.

"I was afraid of that," I said. "I'm sorry. I guess he didn't know how to tell you."

"Tell me what?"

"Is this really a conversation you want to have over a loudspeaker? There are other people waiting to come in out here."

She buzzed me inside. I took the elevator to the seventh floor and walked down the long, wide corridor to the very end. It smelled like disinfectant and fried food and shag carpet. It smelled like retirement.

I knocked on her door but she didn't open it right away.

"Do you have some ID?" she asked, her voice muffled behind the door.

I was glad I'd decided to stay as close to the truth as I could with my story. I wasn't exactly lying, but I was certainly implying a lot more than was true.

I held my Westland employee ID up to the peephole. The ID didn't say anything about me being a security guard, it just had my name, my picture, a barcode, and their badge-and-eagle logo. It must have impressed her, because she slid off the chain, turned the deadbolt, and opened the door.

I expected to see Lauren, the way she'd look if she were an actress playing her older self, after the make-up guy glued on latex wrinkles and rubber jowls and added a few age spots and a stringy, gray wig to obscure her youthful, sculpted beauty. But underneath all that applied age, I knew her intense eyes would shine through, revealing the woman underneath it all, the one that time, real or imagined, couldn't hide.

So, I was startled by the matronly old woman who faced me, her gray hair tied up in a bun, wringing her hands under her grandmotherly bosom. I looked for Lauren's intensity in her eyes, but if it had been there, I wouldn't have had to look for it.

She had the flat gaze of a trout.

If there was an actress underneath that aged skin, she had long ago become the woman she was playing. It was hard to imagine that Lauren had sprung from her loins, or that she'd ever had loins at all.

"I tried calling Cyril while you were on your way up," Mrs. Harper said, "but there was no answer."

"I wish you'd been able to reach him," I lied. "He could probably explain himself better than I can. But I'll try. May I come in?"

She stepped aside and let me walk in past her. Oprah was muted on the TV, the kind that was designed to look like a piece of carved-wood furniture, with built-in drawers and molding. There were framed, family photos on top of the TV and on most of the walls.

"Did you leave him a message?" I asked.

"Yes," Mrs. Harper took a seat on the couch.

"Good," I sat down in a chair facing her. Now Cyril Parkus would know I was in Seattle and what I was doing. The best I could hope for was to get as much information as possible from her before he called back. I wouldn't get a second chance. "I'm assuming you're familiar with the circumstances regarding your daughter's death."

"It wasn't a death," she replied. "It was a suicide. I don't see what there is to investigate."

"For starters, why did she do it?"

"Only she knows."

"Can you live with that? Mr. Parkus can't. He needs to understand. She didn't leave a note and, as far as he knew, your daughter was very happy."

"Lauren wasn't my daughter," she said, looking away from me, "though I certainly loved her as if she was. Even so, I think Cyril has engaged you in a hopeless pursuit that will only prolong his pain. And mine."

Mrs. Harper wasn't her mother. That explained why I couldn't see a trace of Lauren in her face. I marveled at my rapidly-developing detective instincts. I would have to learn to pay more attention to my first impressions.

"What was your relationship with her?" I asked.

Mrs. Harper looked at me suspiciously. "Didn't Cyril tell you?"

"I'd rather hear it from you," I stalled, scrambling to come up with a bullshit explanation. "When I get the story secondhand, all I'm told are the broad strokes and none of the important details."

"It's irrelevant," Mrs. Harper said. "Whatever tormented her was part of her life in Los Angeles."

I could see that she still needed more convincing and time was ticking away. I took a deep breath and leaned towards her, resting my elbows on my knees. I had to show her how serious and competent I was.

"Suicide investigation is my specialty, Mrs. Harper. It's been my experience that it isn't any one thing that makes someone take her own life—but rather an accumulation of events over a long period of time. They eventually build into one, overwhelming presence that permeates every moment of their lives—until there seems to be only one escape. *Death*."

That last word hit her like a slap, which is what I intended. I gave it my best James Earl Jones delivery, as heavy and throaty as I could, then I let the word hang in the air between us, to reinforce the gravity of the situation.

"My job is to track down those scattered events and try to determine how they became something the person could no longer live with."

It sounded like the intro to a TV series: *The Suicide Sleuth*. It might be hard to squeeze in enough sex and action to distract people from the morbid subject matter, but the exciting main titles were already playing in my head.

I looked her in the eye.

"I think we both know that whatever haunted Lauren didn't start in Los Angeles," I added. "It started a long time ago."

Mrs. Harper nodded, tears rolling down her cheeks. I'd gotten to her.

"I thought we'd saved her, that she'd put those horrible

years behind her," she said. "But I see now that I was fooling myself. I see that no matter how much joy or love comes into your life, you can never erase the past."

I tried to hide my excitement. I tried to look caring, concerned, and patient. I tried to look like a guy who wasn't afraid that Cyril Parkus might call at any moment and ruin everything.

"Tell me all about it," I said.

And so she did.

Chapter Sixteen

$$\diamond \quad \diamond \quad \diamond$$

It took her about twenty minutes to lay out the whole story, fighting tears as she remembered it all again, the hope and the happiness and then the pain.

And while she spoke, I wanted to pull out one of the pictures I had of Lauren, to see if the expression on her face, the look in her eye, would slowly reveal their meanings to me as I learned more about her.

The story began about twenty years ago.

Mona and Brock Harper lived in a big house in Bellevue, across the lake from Seattle. He was a lawyer in the shipping industry and frequently entertained clients in his home, from private dinners with a few individuals to large banquets and garden parties.

The Harpers were always looking for dependable domestic help, but they went through maids almost as fast as they went through cocktail napkins. One day, a young woman answered their advertisement for a cleaning lady. She was conscientious, worked fast and efficiently, and clearly had experience. Her name was Lauren, and although she said she was eighteen, Mrs. Harper wasn't fooled.

Still, good cleaning women were hard to find, and not only that, but Lauren was polite, well-mannered, and a perfect hostess when called upon to serve guests at the

Harpers' many social gatherings.

Lauren was also bright and inquisitive. More than once Mr. Harper found her in the library, after her work was done, reading from his leather-bound collection of classic literature, something he'd never done. The books were bought by their decorator, strictly for show. But it pleased Mrs. Harper that Lauren was finding the décor useful. It revealed the maid had intelligence and a desire to better herself.

Mrs. Harper decided to save her.

One night, on his wife's orders, Mr. Harper followed Lauren after she finished work and discovered that Lauren was an orphan, living in a squalid Seattle tenement with a bunch of "runaways, junkies, whores, and radicals." As far as I know, he didn't become a private eye after that. I guess he didn't get the same thrill out of surveillance that I did.

They immediately brought Lauren back to their home, offering her a job as a live-in housekeeper. Lauren settled into the maid's quarters off the laundry room and continued her exemplary work. Meanwhile, Mr. Harper tried to try and find out something about their secretive, but dependable, housekeeper, but to no avail. After a month or two, the Harpers sat Lauren down and told her if she was going to live in their home, she would have to trust them as they had trusted her. She had to tell them the truth about herself.

So, she did.

Lauren admitted that she was only fifteen, and that she was a runaway, but that no one was, or ever would be, looking for her. She said her mother was a junkie who "sold her body," as Mrs. Harper put it, for drugs and money. Lauren didn't know who her father was. The man her mother lived with for years was a drug dealer who sexually molested Lauren whenever her mother wasn't available for him, and sometimes even when she was. Her mother knew about it and didn't care.

Lauren figured her only way out was to either kill them, or run away. She chose to run, because she wasn't about to throw away her life for those two shitheads.

I had a hard time believing the entire hard luck story. To me, the only part that rang true was the drug stuff, because it connected her to Arlo Pelz, whom I'd just learned from Jolene was a seller and a user.

I was very pleased with myself. Through shrewd and dogged detective work, I'd just landed a big clue about where Lauren and Arlo's lives intersected. What I didn't know yet was exactly how. The story Mrs. Harper was telling me certainly wasn't blackmail material, at least not that version. Lauren had risen from a tragic childhood and bettered herself.

Hell, if that story had come out, it would probably have raised Lauren's stature among her fundraising-for-charity social set.

No, the truth had to be something much worse. Maybe Lauren wasn't as clean and wholesome as she'd portrayed herself to the Harpers. What if she'd been an addict and a whore, and Arlo knew it? Worse, what if Arlo could prove it? That might have been something so shameful that Lauren couldn't live with it.

That theory worked, except for one thing. It didn't explain how Cyril Parkus knew who Arlo was, or if he didn't exactly know Arlo, how he recognized his face.

While I was mulling the possibilities, Mrs. Harper went on with her story. I have to confess I was only half-listening at that point, and probably missed some important details.

The upshot was that the Harpers virtually adopted

Lauren. They hired a new maid and Lauren was promoted to surrogate daughter. Somehow, Mr. Harper pulled off some legal magic and enrolled her in the local high school under their name. They told their friends she was a "tragically orphaned" niece they'd adopted. I don't know what lie they told their family, but whatever it was, it worked. No one questioned anything then and hadn't since.

"She blossomed in school," Mrs. Harper said. "She made us so proud. Straight As."

"That's wonderful," I said, eager to go now that I'd found what I needed. There was just one, last thing. "Did she ever mention Arlo Pelz?"

"No," she replied.

I showed her a picture of Arlo, a close-up I took that day on the pier.

"Ever seen him before?" I asked.

She shook her head. "Who is he?"

"A drug dealer."

"Haven't you been listening?" Mrs. Harper stood up, clearly angry. "Lauren escaped from that world. From the day she stepped into our home, that life ended and her new one began."

"Apparently not," I replied.

Mrs. Harper marched over to the wall of family photos and pointed at one of them. "Here she is getting the honor roll. Here she is on the swim team. The debate team. The school newspaper."

She pointed at photo after photo to prove her point. "Does this look like a woman who has anything to do with drugs?"

I looked at the picture. Six teenage girls standing around a printing press, their aprons covered with ink. Not one of them was Lauren.

In fact, Lauren wasn't in a single one of the photos on that wall. I turned to Mrs. Harper and studied her. This crazy woman had created an entirely false, perfect world and inserted her vision of Lauren into it. She'd even gone so far as to put up fake childhood photos on the wall. I could only imagine what Lauren's teenage years had really been like.

"Mrs. Harper, I don't know who that girl is, but she isn't Lauren," I said. "Why don't we start over, with the real story?"

Mrs. Harper looked at the photo, then back at me, then started to speak again, stammering, talking so fast, the words tripped over themselves. "Oh, no! You've got it wrong. You didn't know. This is her. This is Lauren. It's her before."

"Before?"

She grabbed my arm and dragged me over to another photo, of herself, a man I presumed was Mr. Harper, and a teenage girl, taken in front of an old Ford Mustang. I looked into the girl's eyes and I shivered.

"This is a picture of us, a few weeks after Lauren graduated from high school," she said. "Brock bought that car for her as a graduation gift, but it was really more for himself. He'd always wanted a sports car."

She sat down on the couch again. I stayed where I was, looking at the photo again. The same girl was in all of them. I'd never see her before. But I knew her.

"Brock used any excuse to drive that damn car. He was always going on a quick trip to the grocery store for things we didn't really need and asking Lauren if he could borrow her car. Lauren always went with him," Mrs. Harper wiped away fresh tears and struggled to continue. "The police say he was driving fifteen miles over the speed limit when a station wagon pulled out in front of him. He swerved, lost control of the car. It rolled over a dozen times. Brock was killed. Lauren was thrown clear, but she broke her arm, her ribs, and smashed up her face pretty bad."

I stared at the family portrait. Lauren's eyes stared back at me from another person's face, the girl in all those photos.

I took out my picture of Lauren and held it beside the framed photo. It was the same person, only one of them was wearing a mask. I looked at Lauren's picture, her face finally revealing its meaning to me.

No wonder I thought Lauren's beauty looked sculpted. No wonder Carol looked at the pictures and saw a woman who'd had a lot of work done.

We both saw through one of Lauren's secrets and blew it off. How many other secrets had been revealed to me that I'd ignored?

Suddenly, a strange thought occurred to me.

My hand started to shake. To hide it, I put my picture of Lauren back in my pocket and left my hand there.

"Mrs. Harper," I asked, hearing a tremble in my voice, "You wouldn't happen to remember which high school Lauren went to?"

"Of course I do," she said. "Marcus Whitman."

The same school Jolene went to. The school that had a reunion the day Arlo suddenly disappeared.

People, places, and events were colliding in ways I could never have imagined and had an even harder time trying to understand. But all I could do was my part, to connect the obvious dots as they appeared, even if I couldn't see the shape I was creating.

"Do you know if Lauren ever went to one of their reunions?" I asked.

"She got an invitation, but wasn't able to make it," Mrs. Harper said. "Since she wasn't going to attend, the reunion people asked me for a recent picture of Lauren and some news about her life to put in a newsletter they were going to give out at the party."

"Did you give them a picture?"

"No, that wouldn't have been right. I just told them how well she'd done, and how she'd raised so much money for charity in Los Angeles," she replied. "What does this have to do with Lauren's suicide?"

Everything—I just didn't know how yet. A few more questions might have helped me, but I didn't get a chance to ask.

The phone rang.

I immediately headed for the door. "I better be going now, Mrs. Harper; you've been a tremendous help."

"Wait, that could be Cyril," she said, rising from the couch.

"Tell him I'm on the case."

I was out the door and running down the hall by the time she answered the phone.

Chapter Seventeen

✧ ✧ ✧

I went to dinner at a Home Town Buffet off the freeway between Seattle and Snohomish. I piled my plate high with fried chicken, macaroni, chow mein, tater tots, and corn on the cob and took it back to my booth.

While I ate, I looked at the people around me. They all looked suspicious. They all looked like people with secrets.

And when they looked at me, they probably thought I was one of them. Just another average person trying to eat as much as he could for six dollars and ninety-nine cents.

They didn't know that I was a private detective. They didn't know it was my job to see through them, to find out what they didn't want anyone else to discover.

I wondered what they would do if they knew.

I felt like the hero of one of those old World War II movies where a rugged soldier, like Jose Ferrer or Alan Ladd, parachutes into occupied France to carry out a deadly mission. I wasn't sitting in Home Town Buffet, I was in a small café in Bordeaux, and all the other tables were filled with German soldiers. When I talked to the waitress, would subtle mistakes in my French reveal me? Would I die at the table, doomed by a flawed past participle, before I even began my mission?

"Are you done with your plate?" the waitress asked. Her

name was Dede. A sticker on her shirt told me to ask about the senior citizen specials.

I saw the Nazis at the next table eyeing me over their teriyaki chicken wings and tacos. I tried to remain casual.

"Are you serving the mini-corn dogs tonight?" I asked Dede.

"Only on Tuesdays," she replied. "May I take your plate?"

I nodded. The people at the next table looked away, uninterested.

I would live, at least for the moment. They thought I was one of them. Only I knew that I wasn't any more and I was damn happy about it.

I grabbed a fresh plate and got myself some cinnamon buns while they were still hot.

I called Carol as soon as I got to the motel room. It was a good thing I did, because she was about to call the police.

I told her what I'd learned, hoping that since Carol was smarter than me, she might see stuff that I'd missed. I left out the part in my story about telling Jolene which motel I was staying at, and the idea I stole from a book I'd read. I figured there was no sense getting Carol worried. She didn't know yet how cool and professional I'd become, though I hoped telling her about my day at least gave her a hint.

I told her my theory, that Arlo and Lauren were both involved with drugs, and that he knew her before she ran away from home, disappeared, and got a new face. Arlo probably forgot all about her, until the fateful day his ex-wife Jolene got invited to her high school reunion and showed him her yearbook. He must have seen a photo of Lauren and shit himself. Then he read the "Where Are They Now?" newsletter, saw how she'd married a wealthy man and become an active fundraiser for charity, and saw a way to make himself some quick cash.

"Here's a guy, a loser fresh out of prison, who lucks into a woman's deep, dark secret," I said. "If it wasn't obvious that Lauren was rich, Arlo might have just laughed it all off. Instead, he took a plane to LA to soak her for as much as he could. Only he pushed her too hard and she dived off an overpass."

"But you still don't know what the deep, dark secret is," Carol said, "except that it has to do with drugs."

"Arlo was a drug dealer; Lauren's mother and her boyfriend were addicts. At least that's the self-serving story Lauren told the Harpers," I replied. "Now that I've had some experience as a liar, I've discovered the most convincing lies are based on truth. So, I'm assuming there's some truth to the story, only I don't think Lauren was the wholesome, innocent victim or Arlo wouldn't have anything on her."

"Maybe Lauren's mother wasn't the addict," Carol said. "Maybe it was Lauren. And maybe her mother's boyfriend didn't seduce Lauren, maybe it was the other way around, so she could get her hands on his drugs."

"Where does Arlo fit into that?"

"Maybe Arlo was her boyfriend," she said. "Maybe he didn't like her fucking her mother's boyfriend to get drugs."

"Or maybe Arlo was the one who put her up to it, to get drugs for both of them," I added. "Only Arlo began to think Lauren was enjoying doing Mommy's boyfriend too much and maybe wasn't sharing all the dope she got. So, Arlo gets pissed, and tells Lauren's mother what's going on."

"Or arranges for her mother to catch them in the act."

And then it hit me. It was so obvious.

"No, he did better than that," I said. "He took *pictures*."

"Yeah," Carol said softly.

That was it. We both knew. It all fit.

"So, Lauren has to run, because her mother, or the boy-friend, or both of them want to wring her neck," Carol said. "She ends up in a dive in Seattle, lucks into a job with the Harpers, and reinvents herself. She even gets a new face. After a while, it's almost like none of it ever happened, or if it did, it was to a totally different person."

"Until one day," I said, "Arlo Pelz shows up at her door with the pictures and it all comes back to haunt her."

"It makes sense," Carol said.

"That doesn't mean that's what happened."

"It's probably close enough," she said.

We tried knocking around a few other scenarios, but none of them worked as good as that one. It was fun talking about them anyway. We were really enjoying the call.

Two weeks ago, all she had to tell me was office gossip about people I didn't know or care about. Even so, that was more than I usually could contribute to a conversation. Not much happened on the night shift in a guard shack. Now we were discussing blackmail and ex-convicts and drug dealers and secret lives.

Then Carol told me what she'd been doing at work, only for the first time I was interested. She'd been so revved up by the credit stuff she'd found on Arlo that she had to do something more. So, she sat down at her computer and found a couple dozen websites that searched public records and other databases for personal information about people. She didn't find out anything more about Lauren, but she thought that now, based on what I'd told her, she might be able to dig up more on Arlo Pelz. She'd start with the Washington State Department of Corrections and work backward from there.

"You don't have to do that," I said.

"I want to," she said. "I'm enjoying this. Besides, it's the first thing we've really done together."

"No, it's not," I said slyly.

"It's the first thing that doesn't involve a TV, a pizza, or a bed."

Hearing her talk that way, I began to think seriously about starting a detective agency of my own. I'd do the exciting legwork, including the car chases and shoot-outs, while she did all the dull research, cleaned up the office, and fucked my brains out.

It sounded like a dream, only it wasn't anymore. I was most of the way there. All that was left for me to do was win a houseboat in a poker game and I'd have the Travis McGee lifestyle I dreamed of, with some minor alterations. I wasn't interested in rescuing those "wounded birds." For some reason, I didn't have any desire to do that part any more. Carol was enough for me and certainly more than I deserved.

"I love you, Carol."

The words were out of my mouth before I knew I said them. And then, realizing what I'd done, I quickly added a friendly chuckle, so the remark would be taken casually, lightly, maybe even forgotten, shrugged off as just a tongue-in-cheek compliment to a chum. But like I said, Carol was smarter than me.

"I know you do, Harvey," she said, surprising me with the matter-of-fact tone of her voice. "I've known for a while. I was beginning to wonder, though, when it would occur to you."

I swallowed. I fidgeted. I shifted the receiver to my other ear.

"How long have you loved me?" I asked.

"You're the detective now," she replied. "You figure it out."

There was a long moment of silence. I found myself imagining what she was wearing, where she was sitting, the expression on her face. For that moment, I didn't give a shit about Lauren Parkus or her secret or why she killed herself. I wanted to go home and investigate this new mystery.

"Goodnight, Harvey," she said softly. "I'd better hear from you tomorrow or I'm calling the police."

It might have been the nicest thing anybody ever said to me.

I hung up the phone, closed the drapes, and turned off all the lights. I pulled a chair over to the window so I could peek between the drapes and not be seen. Then I sat down in the chair, took out my gun, and set it on the table next to my can of Diet Coke.

I sat there like James Bond in that scene from *Dr. No* and the one thirty-five years later in *Tomorrow Never Dies*. Just a man in a chair with his drink and his gun, waiting for danger to arrive.

It was a longer wait than I expected.

I was driving a '50s T-bird convertible down the Las Vegas Strip. I made a left turn at the Desert Inn, and drove around back to my place.

I drove into the garage, which was also my living room and my office. You'd think a private eye living and working out of his garage would be pathetic, but it was actually very cool.

One of the things that made it cool was my assistant Carol, who had breasts the size of watermelons, really big watermelons, and was waiting for me with a tropical drink.

I climbed over the door of my car instead of opening it. It was a lot more trouble, but it was one of the carefree, cool things I did that made me irresistible to women.

"The casino called for you, Dan. They've got trouble."

"What kind of trouble?"

She showed me a picture of Lauren.

"They say she's gonna jump, unless you can help her," Carol said.

I took the drink and downed it in one gulp and suddenly I was on the roof of the Desert Inn, standing a few feet behind Lauren, who stood on the edge, her back to me, the wind whipping her dress.

I approached her slowly. "You don't have to do this."

"Arlo is back. He is going to tell them everything."

"I'll find him," I said. "I'll stop him."

"That's not going to change anything."

"Your secret will be safe," I said. "No one will know anything."

She turned her head and looked right at me. Her gaze was blinding.

"I will," she said. "I can never forget it now."

And then she jumped.

Chapter Eighteen

$$\diamond \quad \diamond \quad \diamond$$

I'm not sure exactly which sound woke me up. It was either Lauren's body hitting the pavement or the explosion from the motel across the highway.

I whipped open my blinds and saw flames engulfing the room I'd rented at the Sno-Inn Motel and licking the hood of my rented LeSabre, which I'd parked right out front.

It was a huge fire, so hot I could feel it from fifty yards away, behind a pane of glass. And I could hear it, howling in the night, embers snapping in the cold air like cicadas on PCP.

Even so, I still had a hard time believing it. This didn't happen in real life. This didn't happen to me. But that was my room and my car on fire. And once the reality sunk it, I was angry at myself, because I'd slept through it.

I'd missed my chance to catch Arlo by surprise when he came to hurt me. I'd missed the moment of glorious satisfaction when Arlo realized how I'd tricked him, and how much smarter I was than he'd ever be.

I'd missed my sweet victory.

I should have been looking out the window when Arlo sped by and lobbed his Molotov cocktail through the window of my empty motel room.

I should have been out there in the street firing my gun

at his Lumina as he sped off. I should have shot out his tires and sent his car careening out of control. I should have dragged him from the wreckage, made a citizen's arrest, and been a hero.

But that wasn't what happened, because I was asleep, dreaming I was Dan Tana in *Vega$*. Dan wouldn't have let this happen.

I looked out the window at the frightened people running out of their motel rooms in their underwear, and the flames igniting the Sno-Inn's wood-shake roof, and I realized something else.

The flames were meant for me.

Jolene told Arlo where I was staying and he went there to kill me. No one had ever wanted to do that before.

I'd assumed that Arlo would try to scare me off with a good beating. My plan was to catch him when he snuck into my room across the street. When he came out, I was going to smack him on the head with my gun, then kick him once or twice after he hit the ground, just so he'd know what it felt like.

I didn't expect Arlo to toss a bomb into my room.

And if I'd been awake when it happened, I know I would have run out in the street without thinking and started shooting BBs at his car. And he probably would have made a U-turn, mowed me down with his Lumina, and laughed about it all the way back to his mobile home.

So, maybe it was a good thing I slept through it.

I took a sip of my flat Diet Coke and watched the motel burn and my rental car get scorched and listened to the sirens in the distance.

Actually, it was kind of cool.

This was the kind of thing that happened to Matt Houston and Jim Rockford and Dan Tana all the time. And now it was happening to me.

The only thing left was to be knocked unconscious and get shot in the arm, and then I'd really be one of the guys; though, to be honest, I wasn't looking forward to either experience.

All in all, this turn of events wasn't so bad. In fact, I decided I should be pleased with myself and my cleverness. The trick I played by renting two motel rooms, and sticking my car in front of the vacant one, had actually worked. I wasn't in the room that was on fire. I was alive and unscathed. I'd outwitted my adversary.

I also knew for certain that I was really onto something, that Arlo Pelz was afraid of what I might know, what I'd *detected.*

Then I realized the most important thing of all.

Now Arlo Pelz thought I was dead.

I took my ice bucket and went outside to join the frightened Sno-Inn guests as they watched their rooms and their belongings burn.

No one noticed me blending in to the crowd; they were all busy watching the flames devour the motel. I moved among them, eavesdropping as they shared their stories with one another about what they heard and what they saw.

A couple people heard a car peeling out just before the fire. One guy actually saw what he thought was a Pontiac or a Chevy speeding away, but no one got a license number. No one saw anything that would lead the police to Arlo Pelz.

The gnomish manager of the Sno-Inn was the biggest help of all in distracting people from the real perpetrator. He was marching in front of the inferno in his underwear, screaming that the asshole motel-owner across the highway was responsible for the blaze. In fact, the enraged gnome had to be restrained by two men from beating up his competitor, a spindly old man who made the mistake of coming over to offer his condolences.

By the time the fire engines showed up, the motel had all but burned to the ground and the fire had spread to the trees, transforming them into enormous torches. While the firefighters battled to keep the fire from spreading into the surrounding forest, and sheriff's deputies moved through the crowd taking statements, I worked on my story.

The ice bucket I'd grabbed on impulse turned out to be an inspiration. Just by carrying it around with me, I looked like a guy in shock. And it made a nice prop for my story, which was that I left my room to get some ice, heard a screech of tires, and then saw my room ablaze.

The deputy asked what I was doing in Snohomish, and if there was any reason someone might want to do me harm. I told him I was here on vacation and that I was a night-shift security guard in a gated community in Southern California. Why would anyone give a damn about me?

I didn't have to sell him too hard on that one.

I could have told him I was investigating the blackmail and subsequent suicide of Lauren Parkus, and that I suspected ex-convict Arlo Pelz, a dark memory from her druggie past, was responsible for this. But like any half-decent private eye, I didn't do that. I wanted Arlo Pelz for myself.

So, for the second time that week, I lied to the law and was surprised how easy it was for me.

I told the deputy I wouldn't be in the Snohomish area very long and gave him my number in LA. He asked if there was anything he could do to help me. I said I still had my wallet in my pocket when I went to get the ice, so I was in decent shape. In fact, I explained, I'd already reserved a room across the street for the night, so they wouldn't have to worry about me. Which was fine by him. He had plenty of other guests a lot worse off than me to deal with.

I managed to get an incident report number from him and the name of the officer who'd be in charge of the investigation to pass along to Swift Rent-A-Car. I had a feeling they'd want more than my word to explain how their LeSabre had become a giant ashtray.

I hung around for another hour or two, looking suitably spooked, watching them douse what was left of the fire, and then slipped back to my room.

I called Swift Rent-A-Car and gave them the bad news. Because I'd taken all the insurance they'd offered, I was off the hook as far as damages went. They asked, hesitantly, if I wanted another car and I passed. I didn't want to press my luck with the company, especially since I couldn't be sure my next car wouldn't meet a dire fate, too. So I rang up one of their competitors, EconoCar, who agreed to send out their courtesy shuttle to pick me up in an hour.

I didn't have much to pack in the meantime. I'd sacrificed a suitcase, my clothes, my shaving kit, and my copy of Anita Shreve's book to the flames, all things that could be easily replaced or forgotten about. All I had left were the clothes on my back, my wallet, a return ticket to LA, a few pictures of Lauren, and my gun.

I had everything I needed.

So, I went and stood outside in the drizzle to wait for the courtesy shuttle. As dawn broke over the top of the smoldering trees, I watched the firemen pick through the smoking rubble where the motel once stood.

The Sno-Inn was gone and all because Harvey Mapes came to town and asked a few questions. I can't really explain why, and I know it's sick, but it made me incredibly happy.

I picked out a blue Crown Victoria from EconoCar that looked just like an unmarked cop car, drove to a hardware store, and bought a sledgehammer and roll of duct tape to replace the ones I lost.

I drove out of town to the muddy road that led to Jolene's mobile home and pulled off into the weeds. I took out the duct tape, dropped the roll around the handle of the sledgehammer, and went the rest of the way on foot.

I took my time, stopping every few moments to listen and look around. When I got to the clearing, I slipped behind a tree, pulled out my replica Desert Eagle handgun, and peered around the edge of the trunk.

Everything was exactly like it was the day before. Even the Lumina was parked in the same spot. The only sound I heard was the half-open front door of the mobile home creaking in the breeze.

My guess was that they were still asleep, and that Arlo accidentally left the door open when he crept back in after fire-bombing the Sno-Inn.

And now he was sleeping soundly, convinced his troubles were over. He was about to find out how wrong he was. Harvey Mapes was ready for payback.

I was light-headed with excitement, my heart pounding. This was the most exciting thing I'd ever done. And the most dangerous. But I had surprise on my side.

The front door was open, so I wouldn't need the sledgehammer. I left it by the tree, took the duct tape, and made a break for one of the stripped cars. I waited a moment, then went forward a few yards to the discarded couch.

And so I went, from tree to junked car to picnic table,

slowly working my way closer, copying moves I saw Don Johnson use a thousand times on *Miami Vice*. I dashed and I spun and I crouched my way to the mobile home and up the steps to the door. I flattened myself against the wall and tried to catch my breath.

This was the big moment. Time to burst in and take Arlo Pelz down. I'd force Jolene at gunpoint to bind Arlo's wrists with the duct tape and then I'd lead him away. I'd do that bit I'd planned earlier, where I'd threaten to execute him unless he talked, and then once he told me everything he knew about Lauren, about the drugs and whatever else, I'd deliver him to the police, where he'd be charged with attempted murder, blackmail, and extortion. Lauren would be avenged and I'd be well on my way to a successful career as a private detective.

All I had to do was step through that door, where Arlo could be waiting with a sawed-off shotgun to blow me in half.

That wasn't going to happen, I assured myself. Arlo thought I was dead. He wasn't expecting any more trouble.

Unless he heard me drive up. Unless he saw my ridiculous Don Johnson dance across the clearing. Unless he knew I was standing right outside his door.

My mouth was dry, my body was covered with sweat, and, much to my surprise, I was hard. I looked down and I could see my erection, poking against my pants.

It had to be the adrenaline, because I certainly wasn't horny, so thinking about grilled cheese sandwiches and dog shit and Roseanne wouldn't make this untimely tumescence go away. I didn't want to stand there and wait for the adrenaline rush to go, because I needed it to overcome my fear and insecurity. I had to go in, hard-on or not.

But did I really want to confront Arlo with a big boner?

153

How could he take me seriously with *that* poking out?

Because, I told myself, you'll be holding a big, fucking gun.

A toy gun, I countered.

Yes, I agreed, but he doesn't know that.

I decided I had a good point. Fuck the boner. It's not like I'd wet myself. The hard-on simply meant I was surging with manhood. Dangerous manhood.

Maybe it would scare him. Maybe it would make him think I got off on the violence. And if it didn't, I could always pistol-whip the son-of-a-bitch. God knows he deserved it.

I took a deep breath.

I eased open the door with the toe of my muddy shoe and spun into the room in a firing stance, my toy gun and my stiff penis aimed directly at Jolene's corpse.

Chapter Nineteen

✧ ✧ ✧

Somebody had shoved Jolene's head through the big-screen TV, slashing her neck open on the jagged, broken glass. There was blood everywhere, only now it was no longer red, but black and flaky.

She was still wearing her bathrobe, which was now drenched in the shit and piss she expelled when she died, which also accounted for the horrible smell that suddenly hit me and the fat horseflies that buzzed around the room.

I started to gag and, without even bothering to check if I was alone, I ran into the bathroom and vomited in the toilet. I kept gagging until there was absolutely nothing left inside me and I was hugging myself in agony, my cheek resting against the rim of the toilet.

My ribs felt as if they'd splintered apart, sending shards of bone ricocheting into my internal organs. The pain was so bad I thought I was going to faint, my face in the toilet.

But in a few minutes, the worst of the pain ebbed, and I reached out to the sink for support and staggered to my feet. I ran some cold water and splashed my face to revive myself. At least my hard-on was gone, and I feared it might never return.

I stood very still.

I could hear the flies buzzing around and the front door creaking.

I was alone. Except that outside the bathroom, and three steps down the hall, there was a corpse in the living room. A woman I knew, who was alive and talking and drinking coffee just twenty-four hours ago, was dead because of me.

No, *murdered*, because of me.

If she hadn't met Harvey Mapes, she'd be alive. She wouldn't be sticking out of a TV set, her body rotting in her own blood, shit, and piss.

The thought made me gag again, and I hunched over the sink, my mouth wide open, but there was nothing left to heave, except maybe what was left of my rib cage.

This was a nightmare. I'd been hired to follow a cheating wife. That's it. Now I was in a mobile home in Snohomish, Washington, with a corpse. This was the life of adventure I'd always wanted but I never thought it would feel, look, or smell like this.

I straightened up, looked at my reflection in the mirror, and ordered myself to leave the bathroom. I couldn't stay here, as much as I wanted to. I couldn't hide from what was in the living room. It had happened. Now I had to deal with it. Coolly. Calmly. Professionally.

The first thing I had to do was make sure I was really alone.

I picked up my gun off the floor and, breathing through my mouth to avoid the stench, stepped out into the hall. I didn't look in the living room. I put it off by checking out the bedroom first. The only thing that'd changed since I'd last seen it was that Arlo's tennis shoes were gone. I checked the closet and behind the bureau. There was no place for Arlo to hide in here, and I was reasonably certain he wasn't outside.

Now there was only one more place I could go.

I put my gun in my holster and, breathing through my mouth, staggered back into the living room. Again, I tried not too look at the body. I studied the room.

My coffee cup was where I'd left it and so was hers. It didn't take a forensic expert to see that she'd died only a few minutes after I was gone.

Arlo must have been hiding outside when I showed up that day and he recognized me. After I left, he must have come in, found out what she'd told me, and got so mad that he smashed Jolene's face into the big-screen TV.

I wondered if he really meant to kill her or if he'd even stuck around long enough afterwards to know that he had. Not that it mattered. Jolene was dead. And Arlo killed her, just as surely as he killed Lauren Parkus.

And I was his unwitting accomplice both times.

I thought about what I should do next.

The right thing to do, ethically and morally, was to call the police, report the murder, and tell them everything I knew.

If I did that, I would probably be charged with something for misleading them about the fire last night and maybe, if they were really sharp, about the accident in Santa Barbara. Everything I did would get back to Westland Security, and they'd fire me. And then there would be the reports in the press, and the embarrassment that came with it, which would be hard to live down and make it difficult for me to get future employment as a security guard, much less as a private eye.

The only good that would come out of calling the police was that it might get Arlo arrested faster for Jolene's murder. But I didn't see the hurry, not if it meant my life would get totally destroyed.

So, I didn't call.

I decided to stick to my mission and bring in Arlo Pelz myself for what he'd done to Lauren. At that point, I could suggest to the authorities that he was responsible for the fire at the Sno-Inn. As for Jolene's murder, by then they'd have discovered her body and, if they hadn't, I could always point them in the right direction without admitting ever having been here myself.

To pull that off, I had to clean things up, so there was nothing that linked me to the crime scene.

I thought back to my conversation with Jolene and tried to remember everything I did and what I'd touched. I'd seen *CSI*, I'd read those Patricia Cornwell and Kathy Reich novels, I knew how they could nail me on microscopic evidence I didn't even know I'd left. Carpet fibers, lint, hairs, dirt particles, footprints, it was almost too much to comprehend. I'd have to just wash down everything.

Which meant that not only would I be removing any trace of myself, but probably important evidence about Arlo being there, too.

There was no way around that. I was sorry Jolene was dead, but I had to look out for myself.

I found a pair of rubber dish gloves draped over the edge of the kitchen sink. They were too small for my hands, but they covered my fingertips, which was all that mattered. I opened a few drawers and cupboards, found plenty of cleanser and Hefty trash bags, and got to work.

I scrubbed down every surface I touched or might have touched. I vacuumed the couch and the carpets. I removed the vacuum bag and I shoved it into the trash, along with my coffee cup. I mopped the kitchen and bathroom floors, then took the sponge off the end of the mop and put it in the trash, too.

When I was done, I was drenched with sweat and my ribs were a row of jagged knives that stabbed me with each breath.

I felt I deserved it.

I gave the mobile home a quick once-over. I'd covered everything I could. The only thing left inside that I might have touched was the high school yearbook, but I was taking that with me. I shoved it in the trash bag for now. Then I remembered my roll of duct tape. I found it on the bathroom floor and stuck it in the bag, too.

The only trace of me that remained now were my footprints and tire tracks outside, and any fingerprints I might have left where I took cover. I grabbed some Lysol spray and a rag and stuck them in the bag, too.

Careful not too look at Jolene again, I carried the trash bag outside and closed the door behind me. I sprayed Lysol on the screen door, the wall, and the handrail along the steps to remove any fingerprints I might have left. I spotted a hose, which I used to wash muddy footprints and any microscopic stuff I might have left on the steps.

I shut off the hose and surveyed the area. I saw footprints and tire tracks in the mud. I didn't know which tire tracks were mine from yesterday, but I could see where I'd crept from the weeds to the front steps. I could also make out a single, unique tire track that began behind the mobile home and went on down the road.

I followed the tire track behind the motor home. It ended beside a discarded gas can and a bunch of empty bottles and beer cans. Arlo might have used Jolene's car last night, but he'd fled on a motorcycle. I walked to the front again and surveyed the clearing.

Although I couldn't remove my footprints from the clearing without creating new ones at the same time, I could make my movements less obvious. I walked all around the clearing again and behind the trees, so by the time I was done, it was impossible to distinguish my footprints, or any particular path I'd taken, from among all the others in the mud. Besides, I planned on ditching my shoes, along with everything else.

Satisfied that I'd done all that I could, I grabbed the bulging trash bag, retrieved my sledgehammer, and crept back to my car, which I'd hoped no one had noticed parked in the weeds. I put my dish gloves in the bag, put the bag in the trunk, and drove off.

Since I had no more leads and no clue where Arlo was, I made a U-turn and headed for Seattle, simply because it was someplace to go. Along the way, I stopped at a drugstore, and washed down a handful of Advils with a half-bottle of Pepto-Bismol; then I went to a Foot Locker outlet and bought a new pair of sneakers. I stuck my old shoes in the trash bag and removed the yearbook, which I slid under the driver's seat. I wasn't ready to look at it yet.

Instead, I found a pay phone and called Carol. I didn't tell her about the fire or about Jolene's murder. I also didn't tell her I was lost, driving around with a trash bag full of incriminating evidence, with no idea where to go or what to do next.

I pretended like I was confident, totally in charge, and just checking in to see if she'd come up with anything.

"I stayed up all night, searching Internet databases for stuff on Arlo Pelz," Carol said, weary but excited. "I think I got some good information for you."

She'd found out which prison Arlo had done his time at, the date of his trial, and the names of his public defender, his prosecutor, and the investigating officers. None of that struck me as particularly useful at the moment, but

I thanked her anyway. Then she told me she'd discovered one other piece of information. Arlo was born and raised in Deerlick, Washington, just thirty miles north of Spokane, which was where he'd been arrested for his drug activities.

Now I had someplace to go. There was no guarantee that Arlo would go running back home after killing his ex-wife, but it was a place to start. If he wasn't there, hiding among family and friends, I might at least come up with something that would help me find him.

I thanked her again and told her I'd call when I got settled.

"What is it you're not telling me?" she asked.

I thought about it, and then said: "I love you."

It came out stilted, awkward, and forced, but it was such a struggle to say it this time, I didn't have the energy to dress it up.

"I appreciate the effort that went into saying that," she said. "But that isn't what I meant."

I knew what she meant. She meant the fire. She meant Jolene. I hated her for knowing me so well and, at the same time, if I'd told her I loved her right then, it wouldn't have come out stilted at all.

Deerlick was so small, it barely merited a dot on the roadmap, and even then, it was the smallest dot you could register with the naked eye. According to the map, the town was clear across the state, almost a straight shot on I-90 and a solid six-hour drive away from Seattle.

But it took me a lot longer. There were a lot of reasons for that. For one thing, I drove slowly because I'd never traveled that stretch of highway before, or any road in central Washington State, and I didn't want inadvertently to take the wrong fork in the darkness and end up in Peshastin, Wenatchee, Ephrata, Moxee City, or some other strange-sounding place. I also didn't want any highway patrolmen to notice me.

The other thing that slowed me down was that I got off the Interstate at just about every exit that promised gas, food, or lodging. I got off to find out-of-the-way garbage cans to dump a few items from my Hefty bag of incriminating evidence. Dish gloves in Hyak, a coffee mug in Kachess Lake, a mop-head in Cle Elum, a vacuum bag in Thorp, my old sneakers in Kittitas. I spread bits of Jolene's trailer across the state as if they were her ashes.

Before I was even halfway to Deerlick, somewhere around midnight, I'd disposed of everything except the memory of Jolene's corpse and the yearbook that was stashed under the driver's seat, both of which I'd managed to put out of my mind for a few hours. I'd been so intent on running and covering up, that I'd avoided thinking about the case entirely.

Not about *the case*. About the suicide. About the murder. About two dead women. About my responsibility for it all.

But alone on that dark road, with no more tasks to complete and several long hours ahead of me before I arrived at the unknown, there was nothing else to think about.

I'd gone my whole life without affecting anyone else's. I never mattered enough. During the day, I slept in my apartment. During the night, I sat in a guard shack. I didn't see many people and I know they didn't see me.

It was fine.

And then I changed that and within days a friend became a lover, a stranger beat me up, a woman killed herself, a building burned down, and a woman got murdered.

Would any of that have happened if I'd just stayed in my shack?

No, probably not.

And then I realized something that should have made me feel sick, that should have made me pull over suddenly to the side of the road, throw open the door of my car, and cough up a layer of stomach lining. But it didn't, which only proved my realization was the inescapable truth.

I wasn't sorry.

I'd puked my guts out back in Jolene's mobile home out of terror and revulsion, not guilt. Maybe I knew it even then and just didn't want to believe it.

Yes, two women were dead. *But I was alive.*

Alive in a way I'd never been before.

If I'd stayed in my shack, yeah, Lauren and Jolene might have lived. And the Sno-Inn Motel might still be open for business. And I might not have a bunch of broken ribs and a stomach eaten away by painkillers.

But I would still be dead.

I learned then that living doesn't come without painful sacrifices, and that they aren't always your own.

When I got too tired to drive any longer, and I felt the car starting to weave, I pulled over at a rest stop somewhere between Moses Lake and Ritzville.

I didn't go to sleep right away. I pulled out the yearbook from underneath my seat, turned on my map light, and flipped through the pages.

The first thing that tumbled out was the "Where Are They Now?" newsletter. There was a nice write-up on Lauren that made her sound happy, successful, and very rich. It was an enticing advertisement for easy money to Arlo Pelz.

I flipped through the stiff, glossy pages of the yearbook and found Lauren's class picture. She had a bright smile, full of hope and enthusiasm, that was in sharp contrast to her eyes, intense even then, hinting at a darkness I didn't see in any of the other teenagers' faces. It was a darkness that was still in Lauren's eyes when she looked at me on the overpass, right before she took a flying leap.

There was nothing in Jolene's picture that hinted at the disappointments and violence in her future. Her face, like most of the others, radiated nothing but boundless expectation and desire. When she leaped into the air in her cheerleading photos—her arms and legs spread, her face arched up into the sky—the borders of the page could barely contain her from soaring free.

A few pages later, alongside another photo of Jolene in liberating flight, was a picture of Lauren, looking slyly at the camera as she emerged, slick and wet, from the swimming pool. It was the women's sports page, the page a hundred horny high school boys undoubtedly jerked off to. I would have. It was a page for dreaming, for looking at a picture of a cheerleader or swimmer or runner and thinking as you came in your fist . . .

She could be mine.

Years later, Arlo Pelz looked at that page and had the same dream.

The next few pages were torn out. I flipped to the index to see what was missing—it was the crew picture of the women's swim team.

I closed the yearbook, slid it back under my seat, and turned off the map light. I spread out across the big, bench seat, shut my eyes, and worked on some dreams of my own.

Chapter Twenty

$$\diamond \quad \diamond \quad \diamond$$

I woke up because I had to piss.

It was still dark outside. The clock on the dash said it was a little after four a.m. I sat up slowly, my back stiff, my ribs aching, opened the door, and staggered across the empty parking lot to the restrooms.

The bathroom reeked of stale piss. It probably hadn't been cleaned in months. I relieved myself at the urinal and trudged back to my car, thinking I might get another hour or two of sleep before hitting the road again.

That wasn't going to happen.

The driver's side door of my car was open, and so was my trunk.

"Hey," I said.

The trunk slammed shut and revealed a man, about six feet tall, wearing a puffy down jacket, flannel shirt, jeans, and a pair of muddy Doc Martens. Seeing the guy scared the shit out of me.

"No fucking suitcases?" he said angrily, looking right at me.

I suddenly realized just how alone I was. I glanced around and noticed a pickup truck at the far corner of the lot, hidden in the shadows. It must have been his. The infrequent traffic on the Interstate seemed a long way off.

And then I remembered who I was, and where I was going, and why I was in that parking lot. I wasn't afraid anymore. I was excited.

"Get the hell away from my car," I said.

"Or what?" He whipped out a switchblade from somewhere inside his jacket and marched toward me, a lopsided grin on his face. "Give me your wallet and your fucking car keys and maybe I'll let you keep your shriveled little balls."

I made like I was reaching into my back pocket for my wallet and pulled out my gun. He froze, his eyes wide with shock, and then he forced a smile.

"Well, fuck me," he said. "I guess this makes us even."

"Not unless you've got a semi-automatic handgun hidden up your ass," I said. "Then again, you'd have to get to it first."

Now that I had my gun out, I wasn't quite sure what to do next. A hundred tough-guy scenes from a thousand TV shows and movies seemed to run through my head at once. And they all made me realize just how important this moment was for me.

"Drop the knife," I said.

"This is my special knife. I got it in 'Nam." He just stood there, smiling, as if I wouldn't notice he was twenty years too young to have been in Vietnam. "What if I put it in my pocket and I just walk away, no harm done?"

"You could," I said.

He retracted the blade and his hand started towards his pocket.

"But you'd better ask yourself a question first," I said. "Do you feel lucky today?"

His smile began to waver and his hand, the one with the knife, stopped before reaching his pocket.

"Well, do you, punk?" I grinned.

I probably sounded more like Bart Simpson than Clint Eastwood, but the props and the atmosphere more than compensated for it. From the way he looked at me, I could tell he'd decided I was crazy. He dropped the knife.

"This was a setup," he said. "You're one of those psycho-assholes who goes looking for trouble."

"What if I am?" I asked, motioning him towards me with my free hand. "Walk this way until I tell you to stop."

As he came towards me, I moved off to one side, and we made a little circle, until I was near my car and he ended up where I'd been standing before.

"Stop right there and empty all your pockets," I said, "then pull them out so I can see them."

"Fuck you."

"You want to make this hard?" I shrugged and aimed my gun at his groin. "Go ahead, make my day."

He must have seen something in my eyes, because he quickly held up his hands in submission. "Okay, okay, I'll empty them."

He hesitated for a moment, then slowly reached into his jacket. First one wallet, and then another, and then another, hit the ground. Then watches, necklaces, and some car keys. Then he got to his pants; out came some condoms, some loose change, and another wallet, which I figured was his.

I shook my head at him. "You've been a bad boy."

"No worse than you, motherfucker."

I grinned again. I liked that he thought I was tough. But the truth was, if I didn't have my fake gun, by now I probably would have given him my car keys, my wallet, and been sobbing for mercy while he butt-fucked me into the pavement.

As much as I was enjoying the moment, I didn't want to

press my luck. If I stayed much longer, I was afraid the guy would see my gun in the right light and realize it was a fake and kill me with his bare hands. Or somebody would drive in, see me with the gun, and think I was the criminal. And if I was really unlucky, that somebody would be a highway patrolman.

"I want you to crawl into the bathroom, then lie face down on the floor with your feet sticking out the door so I can see them."

"No fucking way I'll crawl for you or anybody else," he said. "You're gonna have to shoot me, asshole."

I sighed. "Works for me."

I aimed at his head.

He immediately dropped to his knees and glared at me. I grinned at him.

"A man's got to know his limitations," I said. "You can thank me for showing you yours. Start crawling."

He turned around and began to crawl towards the bathrooms, his butt facing me. "You better hope I never see you again, motherfucker."

I ran up and kicked him in the stomach, and when he hit the ground on his side, I kicked him twice in the head. He went limp and lolled on his back. I wasn't sure if he was faking it until I heard his bladder empty against the inside of his pants. I was certain he was unconscious then. No one goes that far to be convincing.

I pushed him onto his stomach, rushed to my car, and got out the roll of duct tape. I hog-tied him with the tape, checked his pulse to make sure I hadn't killed him (though I don't know what I would have done if I had), and left him there with his stolen goods. If he didn't get arrested, and somehow managed to get away, he would certainly think twice about robbing someone else at a deserted rest stop.

"You'll rue the night you met Dirty Harvey," I hissed at him. It was the first time I'd ever said *rue* to anybody, whether they were conscious to hear it or not.

I picked up his car keys and his knife and drove off in a hurry.

A half-mile away, I tossed his things out the window and smiled to myself, a smile that lasted for the next two hours.

I considered the experience at the rest stop good practice for the day I'd meet Arlo Pelz again, a day I hoped would come very soon.

I arrived in Spokane at daybreak. It didn't impress me much as a city. If it was worth visiting, somebody would have set a TV series there by now.

It struck me as the kind of place where everybody drove a pickup with a camper shell and owned at least one pair of overalls. There were plenty of old buildings downtown, but I was never interested much in architecture.

I followed I-90 through the city and then drove up Division Street, a row of fast-food franchises that would become the northbound 395 and take me to Deerlick.

As I drove past Riverfront Park, I could see the skeletal remains of the big tent that was the centerpiece of the 1974 World's Fair. It was certainly no Space Needle. That should tell you something about the city's character.

I guess they built a big tent as their enduring landmark, instead of a huge camper shell, because they didn't have the money to erect the giant Ford pickup to go with it.

I only had one set of clothes left after the fire, and I'd just spent the night in them. So I stopped at a Wal-Mart and bought a few shirts, some underwear and socks, and two pairs of pants. I also bought a denim, letterman-style jacket to hide my gun and holster, some toiletries, a nylon gym bag, and a fresh Ace bandage for my ribs.

After making my purchases, I stopped at a Shell station and used the restroom to clean up, put on my new bandages, and change my clothes. I dumped my old clothes and bandages in the trash bin and hit the road.

I felt like a new man.

In fact, I know that I was.

It didn't take long to put Spokane behind me and find myself winding through big stretches of farmland under bright, morning sun. As I passed places like Denison and Clayton and Jump Off Joe, I discovered it didn't require much in Washington State to declare a patch of dirt a town, just a couple gas pumps and a burger place.

By the time I got to Deerlick, I wasn't expecting much and I wasn't disappointed. The turn-off took me down a narrow road past a trailer park, a small cemetery, and an old brick schoolhouse.

The center of the town was dominated by a '60s-era supermarket that might once have been the wreckage of a flying saucer before somebody got the bright idea of building a parking lot around it and selling groceries. The original bright colors of the supermarket had long since faded into shades of gray, the big windows fogged by countless layers of transparent tape used to hang posters for the last forty years.

The supermarket was bordered by Main Street, A Street, and Broadway, which were lined with old storefronts, most of them empty. There was a diner, a beauty salon, a barber shop, a drugstore, a tackle shop, and a post office.

I kept driving down the street, past the town center. There were a few car and boat repair shops, a gas station, and a bar; then the road took you behind the trailer park and around to the highway again.

I made a U-turn and headed back into town, took a right on A Street, and found myself in the residential section. The houses were fifty or sixty years old, the kind with porches and basements and detached garages. Almost all of them had some kind of beaten-up boat on a trailer in the driveway. There were bicycles and kids' toys on the lawns and GM cars parked on the street. I wondered what kind of people lived there and what they did for a living and what would happen to the first person on the block who bought a Japanese car.

I turned around, parked in front of the supermarket, and got out of the car. I was immediately overwhelmed by the smell of sizzling bacon. A hunger I didn't know I had suddenly asserted itself big time.

Like a drooling dog, I followed the scent of bacon to the diner across the street.

The Chuck Wagon was the kind of '50s diner that people in LA buy to renovate into authentic '50s diners.

You lose the real place, with history you can read in the sedimentary layers of grease on the walls, and end up with Johnny Rockets or the Denny's in Camarillo, full of sparkling chrome and shiny, colored tile and a jukebox playing Chuck Berry songs. You end up with a diner the way people think they should have looked, not the way they actually did.

There was nothing shiny about the Chuck Wagon and there was no jukebox. The red-vinyl upholstery in the booths was torn. The linoleum counters and floors were scuffed and chipped. The wood-paneled walls were yellowed by sunlight and steam. There were store-bought bottles of catsup and jars of mustard at every table. The windows had ratty drapes and the ceiling fan twirled lazily.

It was my kind of place.

The Chuck Wagon was about half-full, and just about all the customers were deeply-tanned men wearing faded jeans, faded shirts, and sweat-stained baseball caps that advertised outboard motors or farm equipment. The Evinrudes and Chris Crafts and John Deeres looked at me in my new shirt, new jacket, and new slacks as if I were some kind of alien being the likes of which they hadn't seen since the super-market landed from outer space in 1962.

I smiled feebly and took a seat at the counter. I snatched the one-page, laminated menu from the napkin holder and gave it a quick look.

There were less than a dozen items on the menu: combi-nations of eggs, pancakes, hamburgers, and steaks. On the back there was a list of four homemade pies (apple, pecan, chocolate, and banana cream) and two kinds of ice cream, chocolate or vanilla, to choose from. The prices were cov-ered with white tape and written over by hand in ballpoint pen. There wasn't anything over six bucks. I wanted to try everything.

"What'll it be, sir?" the waitress asked wearily.

I looked up and saw a tired woman in her forties, stuffed into a too-tight, stained white uniform, her hair pinned into a bun. She wore a bra that made her breasts look like air-plane engines, her name stitched in script across one of them.

I ordered the Rancher's Breakfast of eggs, steak, bacon, pancakes, and hash browns, and asked Georgette for an extra-thick chocolate shake to wash it down with.

While I waited for my meal, I watched the short-order cook move piles of hash browns and stacks of bacon strips around the grill, making room for the eggs and pancakes and steaks he was preparing. In between all that, he ladled

oil onto the grill and used an ice cream scooper to dig
butter out of a bucket, dropping the gobs into his frying
pans. It was excruciating, gastronomical foreplay.

By the time Georgette set my plate down in front of me,
I was so hungry I was nearly slobbering. I wolfed the hot
meal down in about ten minutes and immediately ordered
another shake.

It may have been the best breakfast I ever had in my life.

When she brought me the shake, with a dollop of
whipped cream sprayed on top, I was sated and finally
ready to get to work.

"Excuse me," I said, stifling a burp. "Have you seen
Arlo around?"

She looked like I'd slapped her, but she recovered
quickly. I guess she was used to being slapped.

"Who?" she asked unconvincingly.

"Arlo Pelz," I replied, and took a big slurp of the shake
to drown out another burp. "You know Arlo, don't you
Georgette?"

I was aware that everybody in the restaurant had stopped
talking. They were all listening, which was fine with me.
The more people who heard, the better. I wasn't all that
great at detecting, so I figured it would be a lot easier to let
him find me.

"I haven't seen him," she said. "You a friend of his?"

"You could say that." I smiled and leaned over, plucked
a pen from her apron pocket, and started scrawling a note
on my napkin. "If he stops by, maybe you could give him
this for me."

I wrote: *Jolene is really into her TV. She asked me to thank
you. Your pal from the Sno-Inn.*

I read it out-loud in case she lost it, and so everybody
else got my message. I wrapped the napkin around a ten-

dollar bill and put it, and the pen, back in her apron pocket.

"I appreciate it," I said, flashing her another insincere smile.

She dropped my breakfast check on the counter and walked away without bothering to ask me first if maybe I wanted a slice of pie or something.

I took the hint, though I would have liked to try a slice. I gulped down the last of my shake, dropped another ten on the counter, and walked out.

I visited the barbershop, the beauty salon, and the drugstore, and left pretty much the same message at each place. In the post office, I asked the aged clerk behind the counter if he knew where the Pelz family lived.

"There isn't any family left here except for little Billy," the clerk said. "Still lives at their place on A street. Sixteen A Street."

"What about Arlo," I asked. "Seen him around?"

The old man narrowed his eyes at me. "Once, right after he got out of prison. You a friend of his?"

"Not really," I said. "How about you?"

The clerk just turned and walked away, disappearing into the back of the post office.

I walked out and went next door to the tackle shop. They sold fishing poles, reels, lures, hooks, and all kinds of worms, crickets, and maggots. A man sat at the counter stringing a fly. As I got closer, I realized if you drew a line connecting the five moles on his cheek, you could make a lopsided star. I wondered if he knew that.

He looked up at me as I approached the counter. "Can I help you?"

"I'm up here doing some fishing," I said.

"Whatcha interested in catching?" he asked. "Salmon,

trout, perch, bass, mackinaw?"

"Arlo Pelz."

I felt really cool saying that. I don't think Mannix could have delivered it any better.

"I understand he's a bottom-feeder native to these parts," I said.

He stopped working on his lure, stood up, and gave me a hard look. "Are you a cop of some kind?"

I smiled thinly. "Of some kind."

"I haven't seen him."

"Where do you suppose he'd be likely to go, if he came back for a visit?"

He thought for a minute. He wasn't searching for the answer, he was trying to decide if the answer might get him hurt.

"You could check out his place on A Street," the man replied. "Of course, you'd have to get past Little Billy first."

I shrugged as if getting past anyone was easy for me. "Anyplace else?"

"Maybe the woods around the lake," he said. "He used to hang out there a lot when he was a kid."

"Why was that?"

"Same reason kids still do," he replied. "To drink and fuck. He also liked to hide there."

"What was he hiding from?"

"Everybody," he replied. "He used to work in the marina, fixing outboards, before he gave that up to break into homes on the lake. Vacation places, empty most of the time. It'd be months before anyone realized they'd been robbed."

"Where can I find the lake?" I asked.

"It's about ten miles farther up the highway," the man said. "Can't miss it. Big Rock Lake."

I got that chill of creepy realization up my back, only I was missing out on the realization part. I didn't know why the name of the lake sounded strangely familiar to me.

"They got some place to stay the night up there besides the woods?" I asked.

"You can rent a cabin at the Big Rock Lake Resort."

I got that chill again and it bugged me. I thanked the man for his help and left, thinking maybe the fresh air would clear my head.

It wasn't until I'd crossed the street and was halfway to my car that I remembered where I'd heard the name of the lake before.

Actually, I didn't remembering *hearing* it, I remembered *seeing* it. On the peeling, faded sign that hung above Cyril Parkus' fireplace. The sign that said *Big Rock Lake Resort.*

I was so busy thinking, I didn't see the guy sitting on the hood of my car until I was nearly standing in front of him.

And that's when the guy, three hundred pounds of bad karma in a Grateful Dead tank-top and shorts, slid his huge ass off my car and stood up in front of me, resting a baseball bat on his shoulder.

Chapter Twenty-One

$$\diamond \quad \diamond \quad \diamond$$

All the books and TV shows are very clear about what I was required to do in that situation: show no fear and come up with lots of smart ass remarks. I realized right away that acting on my instinct, which was to either run away or beg for mercy, wasn't appropriate.

I tried to exude tough-guy calm which, at that moment, mainly consisted of suppressing my urge to whimper.

"I hear you're looking for my brother," the Neanderthal said, his voice full of menace.

"I was hoping word would get around," I said, letting one hand slip behind my back. "You must be Little Billy."

"You know why they call me Little Billy?"

"Because it's supposed to be humorously ironic, given how big, fat, and stupid you are?"

Little Billy took a step toward me, but I held my ground, not so much because I'd mastered the tough-guy thing, but because I was petrified with fear.

"I got the name because a cop once snapped a billy club in half on my head and still couldn't take me down."

"It's a shame about the brain damage, but at least you got a cute nickname," I said, surprising myself. "Where's Arlo?"

"I don't know." Little Billy grinned. "Then again, maybe I do."

I grinned back: "Tell him I know how he found her and what he had on her. Tell him I want sixty percent of the action or I give everything I know to the cops."

I didn't know where the words and the grin were coming from. Maybe it was that big breakfast that did something to me. Or maybe it was my rest stop performance as Dirty Harvey. Whatever the reason, I was running on pure impulse. I hadn't even stopped to think yet about how everything fit together, how Big Rock Lake connected to drugs, Lauren, Arlo, Cyril, and Seattle.

"What's to stop me from shutting you up with this bat instead?" Little Billy asked.

"Why don't you try and see for yourself?"

I said it with surprising self-confidence, which I really shouldn't have had. In the bright light of day, I couldn't be sure he'd be fooled by my BB gun or that I'd even be able to whip it out before he took off my head with his bat.

But like I said, I wasn't thinking.

I walked past him, expecting to get whacked with that bat at any moment, but to my astonishment, he let me go unharmed. As I walked around to the driver's side door of my car, I noticed the dent his ass had left on my hood and congratulated myself again for taking all the insurance that EconoCar had to offer.

I opened the door and glanced at Little Billy, who stood on the curb, tapping the end of his bat into his palm, staring at me with the flat, dead eyes of a shark.

"I'll be in touch," I said.

I got in and drove off before Little Billy could change his mind about taking that swing at me. My work in Deerlick was done. If Arlo was there, he knew by now that I was, too.

The Man with the Iron-On Badge

★ ★ ★ ★ ★

The Big Rock Lake Resort billboard, which stood along the highway a quarter mile ahead of the turn-off, promised "exciting water sports, great fishing, rustic cabins, and delicious home cooking" over a cartoon of a surprised fisherman getting yanked out of his boat by the gleeful trout on his hook.

I took the turn-off, a gravel road that ended at the Big Rock Lake Resort Store and Restaurant, a large, white, clapboard building that was mostly porch, and built onto its namesake, allowing it to loom a bit over the lake, the dock, and the beach below. On either side of the store, set back from the shore by a dry lawn, were ten identical white cabins, with small porches facing the water.

I parked my car behind a row of railroad ties and got out. The hot, heavy air smelled of outboard motors, lighter fluid, fish guts, and suntan lotion. Most of the cabins looked empty; a few had families camped out front, the kids running around, the sagging mothers basting on chaise lounges, while the pot-bellied fathers knocked back beers and looked for teenage girls to ogle. There were a few water skiers and fishing boats on the small lake, but there didn't seem to be a lot of action. It was the kind of lake where people parked Winnebagos instead of building vacation homes, though there were a few of those, most not much more elaborate than the Big Rock cabins.

I strode up to the Big Rock Lake Resort Store and Restaurant, admiring the sign on the roof. Although it was weathered and peeling, I knew it was newer than the one in Cyril Parkus' living room.

The porch was lined with wooden benches and surrounded the open counter that passed for the store. All the merchandise was on shelves behind the counter, which itself was a glass display case full of melting candy and fishing lures. The restaurant was a screened-in section of the porch that faced the lake, with a hand-painted menu above the counter and an electric fly trap in the corner that snapped every few seconds.

I took a stool at the restaurant counter beside a couple old men smoking cigarettes and nursing mugs of coffee. They looked liked they'd been installed with the stools fifty years ago. A couple kids sat on the bench, staring at the fly trap, letting their Popsicles melt all over their bathing suits as they waited in suspense for another insect to get zapped.

"What'll it be?" asked the man behind the counter, who wore a big apron that had the same cartoon as the highway billboard. He was as jolly as a department store Santa, with a body to match.

I looked at the menu above the counter. The prices had been painted over and changed many times, but the menu remained the same. Burgers, hot dogs, bacon, and eggs, and a combination of them all called the Big Rock Burger.

I'd had a big breakfast, but acting tough gave me an appetite.

"Gimme a Big Rock Burger, please," I said. "It'll bring back memories."

The man immediately repeated the order to someone in the kitchen, which was hidden somewhere in back.

"So you've been here before," the man ventured jovially, as I'd hoped he would.

I nodded with a smile. "When I was a kid." I offered him my hand across the counter. "The name's Harvey Mapes."

He shook my hand enthusiastically. "Tom Wade, pleasure to have you back."

"The place hasn't changed much," I said.

"Just fresh coats of paint," he replied. "Any of the pictures on that wall could've been taken yesterday."

Wade motioned to a wall covered with about a hundred faded snapshots and Polaroids, some framed, some stuck to the paneling with thumbtacks or yellowed tape.

"The fish were a lot bigger then," grumbled one of the old men.

"You can say that again," another old-timer agreed. "Coffee tasted better, too."

Wade laughed and freshened up the old timer's cup. "Maybe if I warm it up, you won't notice."

"The sign out front looks different," I said, as if making a fresh observation.

"You've got a good memory and a sharp eye," Wade said. "The only thing the family that sold me the place kept for themselves was the sign. Sentimental value, I suppose. Couldn't really begrudge them that. I tried to copy the original sign as best I could, but I couldn't get it quite right."

A woman built just like Wade came out and set the Big Rock Burger down in front of me, then stood there expectantly to see if I was satisfied. I took a big bite out of it. It was wonderful.

"You certainly got the Big Rock down right," I said through my mouthful of hamburger, hot dog, bacon, eggs, and cheese. "It's perfection, even better than I remembered."

The woman beamed with pride. "Thank you kindly," she said, then disappeared into the back again.

"That's my wife, Betty Lou," Wade said, smiling after her. "The only thing she loves more than cooking is watching people eat what she makes."

"Where can I find a wife like that?" I asked.

"You can look anyplace but right here!" Wade chuckled good-naturedly and so did I.

I took a few more bites of my Big Rock Burger, then said: "I vaguely remember the people who used to run the place. Their name was Parkus, wasn't it?"

"Josiah Parkus," Wade nodded. "This place was in their family since the early 1900s."

"Then why did they sell it?"

"Too much tragedy, I suppose." Wade took a cloth from his apron and started to absently wipe the countertop. "Josiah's wife Esme killed herself in '74. He woke up one morning and Esme was gone. A few hours later, he found one of their boats floating in the middle of the lake. The anchor was missing."

"Fisherman out trolling for macks snagged Esme's dress in '75," the old man with the coffee said. "Maybe it was '76."

"Their daughter Kelly never really got over it, drowned herself the same way a few years later," Wade said. "That just left Josiah and his son."

"Cyril, wasn't it?" I asked.

Wade nodded. "Neither one of 'em was much interested in running the resort after that, though Josiah stuck it out on his own after Cyril went off to California. When Josiah died, Cyril sold the place to me. We used to run an RV park up at Spirit Lake, but we always envied this outfit."

I finished up my burger and tried to figure out how all of this tied together with what I already knew. After thinking about it for a few minutes, the pieces fit pretty good.

Cyril knew Arlo Pelz because they grew up together, with Arlo probably resenting the hell out of Cyril the whole time. Arlo worked for Cyril's father at the resort marina, fixing outboard motors, and it wouldn't surprise me if Cyril treated Arlo as his employee, too.

After Kelly Parkus killed herself, Cyril went off to California, and Arlo got into drugs, eventually ending up in Seattle, where he met Lauren, who was either a drug addict, a drug dealer, or a whore. Or maybe all three.

Somehow they split up, how or why I don't know. A few years went by. Arlo married Jolene, went to prison for dealing drugs, and when he got out, he stumbled into the discovery that Cyril, wealthy and powerful, was married to a woman with a dark, shameful past her husband probably didn't know about. Arlo guessed Lauren would pay dearly to keep it that way.

Instead, something went wrong.

That something was me, Harvey Mapes.

I uncovered the blackmail scheme and told Cyril about it. Cyril confronted his wife with what I'd found out and then she, unable to deal with the exposure of her ugly past, killed herself.

Now poor Cyril was left to mourn the suicide of yet another woman in his life.

It all made sense. All that was missing were the sordid little details, which I expected to wring out of Arlo once I captured him.

"How about a slice of pie to go with that?" Betty Lou Wade asked, sliding a huge hunk of apple pie in front of me before I could answer.

I smiled back at her. "I don't see how any sane man could refuse."

She beamed again. I dug into the pie. Marie Callender and Sarah Lee had nothing on Betty Lou Wade. I picked up my plate and fork and worked on my pie as I wandered over to the wall of photos.

The snapshots captured nearly identical moments in time, spread out over decades, of people standing in front of the store, posing with their fish, smiling into the lens.

Occasionally, a portion of a parked car or a particular style of clothing would give away when the picture was taken, but otherwise they could have all been shot today.

I saw what probably amounted to tons of dead fish.

I saw the Parkus family, I saw Arlo, and I saw most of the citizens of Deerlick that I'd met, even Little Billy when he actually was little.

And as I stared back through decades, the pie plate slipping from my hands and shattering on the floor, I saw what I got right and what I got wrong, and just how cruel and inescapable fate could be.

Chapter Twenty-Two

$$\diamond \quad \diamond \quad \diamond$$

I rented the cabin closest to the woods for the night, parked my car right behind it, then called Carol from the pay phone outside the store.

I didn't tell her anything that happened to me or what I'd found out. All I said was that I was in Deerlick, asking around for Arlo, and that I'd be staying at Big Rock Lake overnight. I told her I thought Arlo might be in town, but I didn't know for sure.

That last part was the biggest lie of all.

I knew he was there. I felt it as clearly as my own heartbeat.

I gave Carol the number at the Big Rock Lake Resort Store, since the cabins didn't have phones. She didn't ask me why I gave it to her, and I was glad, because she probably would have seen through whatever lie I came up with. The truth was, if she didn't hear from me in a day or two, I wanted her to know who to call first to go look for my body.

I wasn't being morbid or fatalistic, just practical. I had every intention of capturing Arlo and bringing him in to pay for his crimes, but I also knew how badly things could go wrong. Recent experience certainly proved that.

I told Carol I loved her and this time it wasn't hard to

say. It sounded to me like saying it came pretty easy for her, too.

I spent the afternoon sitting on a chaise lounge on the lawn in front of my cabin, right where everybody could see me, drinking Cokes and looking at the lake.

I was surprisingly relaxed, considering what I still had left to do. I guess I was either confident in my abilities or too stupid to realize just how much danger I was in.

Sitting there like I was made me think of an episode of *Maverick*, which starred James Garner as gambler and conman Bret Maverick.

My dad loved that show. There was this one episode where Maverick wins a poker game, then convinces a banker to let him make an after-hours deposit to keep his money safe. The next day, Maverick goes in to get his money and the banker says slyly, "What money?"

See, nobody witnessed the transaction. It's Maverick's word against the banker's, and who is going to take the word of a conman?

So Maverick tells everybody he's gonna get his money back . . . and what he does is, he sits in a rocking chair across the street from the bank and just starts whittling. People walk by every day and ask him, "How's it goin', Maverick? You gettin' your money back?" And every day he says, "I'm workin' on it."

The thing was, while he spent the whole episode sitting in that rocking chair, unnerving everybody by happily doing absolutely nothing, a gang of his conman friends were swindling the banker out of exactly what he owed Maverick.

My dad was a gambler, but mostly he was a loser. Whatever he won at the poker table, when he rarely won, was lost the next day. He never got ahead. I think my dad wanted to be James Garner as Maverick the way I wanted to be James Garner as Rockford.

What did that make me?

I didn't have a gang of conman friends, or anybody else, to help me do what I was going to do that night. So it didn't make a whole lot of sense for me to be sitting there, sunning myself like I didn't have a care in the world. I should have been laying down some clever plan.

I had a plan. It wasn't clever. It wasn't likely to work any better than my dad's bluffs at the poker table.

It didn't matter anyway. I was powerless to control what was going to happen next and I pretty much knew it. What I'd learned over the last few days convinced me that the outcome was inevitable and that I was just doing my pre-destined part.

When the sun set, it started to get chilly. The resort guests slowly drifted back to their cabins. I stayed where I was for a while, listening to the water lapping against the boats tied to the dock and watching the bats skim the surface of the dark lake.

I imagined Esme Parkus on the muddy bottom, her dress swirling around her skeleton, dozens of sparkling fishing lures caught in the tattered fabric.

And I thought about Kelly Parkus, rowing her boat into the middle of the lake late one night, contemplating the same fate for herself.

I got up, strolled over to the Big Rock Lake Resort Store, and walked around the porch into the restaurant.

The day's heat was trapped inside. The electric bug trap snapped and crackled, sending off tiny sparks as one insect after another got zapped. It was almost festive.

I took another look at the photos on the wall. One day, Esme and Kelly Parkus were there, grinning in front of the store, and then they weren't. Time at Big Rock Lake just kept marching on, measured only by all the big fish that didn't get away.

I took a seat at the counter and ordered another Big Rock Burger from Tom Wade.

"Sorry again about breaking the plate," I said.

"Don't worry about it," he said, absently wiping the counter in front of me with a rag.

"Why do you suppose Esme drowned herself?" I asked.

He smiled at me. "Can't get it out of your mind, can you?"

I didn't answer.

"Once you've heard the story, it's hard not to think about it," Wade said. "It's the kind of tragedy that becomes legend. What is it about the lake that draws beautiful young women into its cold depths?"

"But it wasn't the lake, was it?"

"Not entirely."

Wade went back into the kitchen and came back with my burger, setting it in front of me. "Josiah Parkus and his father cut down the trees, cleared the land, and built this store, the docks, and the cabins themselves. They didn't build this place, they *birthed* it. It wasn't a business to them, it was a life. Everything else came second. You follow what I'm saying?"

"The resort was his priority; his wife and kids came later," I said between bites, just to prove I was paying attention.

"And that was the crux of their problem. Esme fell in love with Josiah, not with the lake. But, see, it was a package deal. He'd never leave, so neither could she," Wade said. "Josiah didn't make it easy on her. He expected Esme and his kids to be as devoted to the lake as he was.

Wasn't gonna happen. Esme hated the lake but she loved him. Something had to give, and it sure as hell wasn't gonna be Josiah Parkus."

Wade shrugged.

"So she sacrificed herself to the thing he loved most," I said.

Wade nodded.

I'm not usually so poetic, but something about the stillness of the night, the dark romance of the story, and the crackle of electrified insects brought it out in me.

"I didn't know Esme," Wade said, "but I've heard enough about it from folks who did to believe that's the way it happened. But I knew the kids, I saw the way Josiah worked them, the way he tried to force them to love this place the way he did. He was especially hard on Kelly, maybe because of what happened to Esme. After she died, all those two kids really had was each other. They knew there was no way off this lake for them."

"Kelly found one," I said.

"She didn't really leave, though, did she?" Wade said, inadvertently glancing at the lake below, then catching himself at it. "But she broke the hold Josiah had on Cyril. The boy left, didn't even come back for his father's funeral."

I finished up my burger and pushed the plate towards Wade. "So, are you as hung up on this place as Josiah Parkus was?"

Wade picked up the plate and wiped away the crumbs I'd left on the counter.

"I didn't build it with my bare hands," he said. "I just bought it."

I had another slice of pie, thought about what Wade had told me, then went back to my cabin for the night to wait for Arlo Pelz.

★ ★ ★ ★ ★

The cabin was laid out a lot like my apartment, a combination kitchen and living room in front, and the bedroom and small bath in back.

The walls were covered with sheets of wood paneling, the floors were linoleum. It was furnished with a vinyl couch and a Formica-topped table with some plastic chairs around it. There was a bad painting of a duck on the wall.

Just what you'd expect for forty-five dollars a night.

Considering how Arlo botched things at the Sno-Inn, I was reasonably certain he wouldn't go the fire-bomb route again. This time he'd want to be sure that he'd gotten the job done, and there was only one way to do that.

I messed up the bed and used the pillows to create the vague outline of a person under the blankets. It's an old trick that's been used a thousand times on television, so I figured it must work.

I turned off all the lights, dragged one of the kitchen chairs into the bedroom closet, and sat down, the roll of duct tape on the floor and my gun on my lap. I drew the closet curtain closed in front of me and waited.

I wasn't worried about falling asleep this time. One of the reasons I drank so many Cokes during the afternoon was to tank myself up on caffeine. But when I did start to feel a bit drowsy, I just reminded myself what Jolene looked like the last time I saw her. That sharpened me up real quick.

As I sat there in the closet of that cabin, feeling the night chill seeping through the old boards, smelling the pine of the surrounding forest, I thought about my guard shack. It wasn't a whole lot bigger than that closet, but it seemed a world, and a lifetime, away.

It had been a little over a week since I'd been hired to

follow Lauren Parkus. Before that, I'd never been the victim or inflictor of violence. I'd never seen a person die. And I'd never been in love.

But it seemed to me that all those years, all those nights, of sitting alone in that guard shack was training for this moment. I had no problem sitting in a closet like a suit of clothes waiting to be worn or a box waiting to be opened. I'd learned to sit in a cramped space and wait for something to happen, even if most of the time nothing ever did. I'd become an expert at passivity, at waiting for life to happen rather than going after it myself.

Not anymore.

I thought about Esme, Kelly, and Cyril Parkus, about how it was them against their father and the lake, and what life must have been like for them after Esme died.

It made me think about my mother, my sister Becky, and me, and about my father, who loved to gamble and sacrificed everything for it. I remembered how things changed after my mother ran off, how Becky stepped up and ragged on my dad the same way mom used to, and just as ineffectively.

When I was a kid, I thought we had a uniquely fucked-up family, that nobody else could possibly understand what it was like being abandoned by your mother and left with a father who lived for something he thought was more important than you.

Well, it turned out I was wrong. We weren't uniquely fucked-up, we were just as fucked-up as lots of other families. Cyril Parkus may have been a rich guy in a big house with the stone lions, and I was just the loser in the stucco shack on the other side of the gate, but we were more alike than either of us would have thought.

I wasn't quite sure how to feel about that.

Sitting in that closet, alone with my memories, I was surprised how fast the hours slipped past. It seemed like only a few minutes had gone by when, at two a.m., I heard the soft footfalls in the living room.

Arlo slunk into the room and up to the bed, holding one of those big, serrated Rambo knives in his fist. Knives seemed to be the weapon of choice with criminals in Washington State. He raised the knife over his head, then brought it down with a vengeance, plunging it deep into the covered pillows.

While he was bent over like that, slightly off-balance, I leaped out of the closet behind him, slammed his head into the wall, then smashed his face down on the night stand for good measure, his nose bursting like a water balloon. I let him drop to the floor.

"You aren't much of a criminal mastermind, are you?" I said.

I stomped on Arlo's back, keeping him down while I looked for the Rambo knife. It was still sticking out of the bed. He'd been fooled by the pillow trick. Who says you can't learn anything watching cop shows?

I went to the closet, snatched up my gun and the roll of duct tape, and turned around to see Arlo trying to get up. I noticed he was wearing the same tennis shoes he used on me in Santa Monica. That pissed me off all over again.

I stomped him down, then gave him a swift kick in the side.

"That's for what you did to me in Santa Monica," I said. I gave him another kick and thought I felt something give against my shoe. "That's for Lauren."

Then I grabbed him by the hair, lifting his blood-splattered face off the floor so he could see me. I looked right into his dazed, watery eyes.

"And this is for Jolene," I hissed into his ear, right before I slammed his face into the floor a couple of times. "The rest of your punishment I'll leave up to the law."

I straddled his back, pulled his arms behind him, and bound his wrists with duct tape. Then I taped up his ankles together, grabbed him under the arms, and dragged him into the living room. I propped him up against the couch, set my gun on the table, then pulled out a chair and sat down so I could take a good look at him.

I was momentarily repulsed, not so much by the man in front of me, but by what I'd done to him. Before that guy tried to rob me on the Interstate, I'd never beat up anybody before. I didn't think I could do it. I certainly never thought I'd enjoy it. But I'd never imagined I'd be in a place like Deerlick, stuck in a cabin alone with a murderer.

It wasn't even a fair fight. If it had been, I had no doubt I'd have been the loser. I prevailed because I ambushed Arlo, then kicked the shit out of him when he was down and couldn't defend himself.

It didn't say much about me as a man.

Travis McGee and Spenser would be ashamed of me. More importantly, I suspected Carol would be, too.

Not that it mattered, but Arlo wasn't going to give me a chance to defend myself either, stabbing me to death as I slept. And what I did to Arlo was far less brutal than what he'd done to Jolene or Lauren. Violence was an inherent part of his character; it wasn't in mine.

Maybe it would be now.

Arlo's head lolled on his chest and he drooled blood and mucus onto himself. After a few minutes, he began to groan. He lifted his head up slowly, spat out a big glob of blood and teeth, then tried to focus his eyes on me.

When he spoke, it wasn't easy to understand him, what

with his smashed nose and mouthful of teeth.

"You're the guy who pissed on my money," he slob-bered.

I'd hunted him down, uncovered his scheme, foiled his attempts to kill me, and ultimately captured him, and that was all he had to say. He'd murdered his wife and drove Lauren to suicide and this was how it was going to end.

So much for my evil adversary. My Moriarty.

I looked at him and found it hard to believe that someone so stupid and pathetic could cause so much misery and death. It didn't say much for me, if this guy had met his match.

I thought about terrorizing some answers out of him, like I'd originally planned, but the idea had lost all of its allure. I'd captured him and given him a beating. That was enough. Suddenly, I was tired of the whole damn thing and just wanted to go home.

"I'm going to go and call the police now," I said. "But first I want to know if Little Billy is out there waiting for you."

Arlo didn't say anything.

"You better tell me if he is," I said. "Because if I see him, I'll shoot him dead and say it was self-defense."

I picked up my gun and aimed it at him, so he'd get the point.

"With a BB gun?" Arlo slobbered.

I could have hit him again and felt good about it.

Instead, I taped his mouth shut, tipped him over on his stomach, and hog-tied his arms and legs together. I didn't want him slithering back to his Rambo knife or finding some other way to cut his bonds while I went up to the phone booth.

I looked at my handiwork. It was a good thing I'd had

that highway robber to practice on. The police might not be so impressed, but I couldn't see how they could call me anything but a hero.

I wished I'd felt more excited about capturing Arlo, but I figured that would come later, once I'd put some time between me and everything that had happened, once it didn't seem so ugly and it became just a story I told.

I eased open the front door and peered out into the darkness. If Little Billy was out there, he was doing a good job of blending into the surroundings.

My gun held at my side, I closed the door behind me and cautiously stepped off the porch, careful to peer around the edge of the cabin first.

Then something grabbed me by the ankles and the ground came rushing up to my face. I instinctively reached out my hands to break my fall and my gun flew out of my grasp.

I slapped against the ground hard, my arms taking most of the impact. I was about to scramble for my gun when my head exploded and I died.

Chapter Twenty-Three

$$\diamondsuit \quad \diamondsuit \quad \diamondsuit$$

You don't dream when you're unconscious. It's not like sleep. And when you wake up, you wish you hadn't.

It was still dark.

At first that was all I was aware of, beyond the pulsating pain in my head. Then I was aware of being alive, which confused me and gave me an incentive to get past the agony and focus my eyes.

After a minute or two, I was able to sharpen the blur enough to tell I was lying on my back on the cabin floor. I was afraid to lift my head up, because it felt like the floor was the only thing holding my brain inside my skull.

I turned my head a tiny bit and saw my gun on the table, beside the roll of duct tape. Neither Arlo nor Little Billy seemed to be around.

So I lay there, waiting for some sensation besides pain to return, pondering my predicament.

The last thing I remembered was going outside to call the police. Someone was hiding under the porch, knocked me down, and hit me on the head with something.

My guess was a large baseball bat.

What I couldn't figure out was why I was still alive. Arlo came to kill me, and I'd given him a beating and trussed him up with duct tape. If anything, he had more reason to kill me now than he had before.

So why didn't he finish the job?

Maybe he was getting ready to. Maybe this was the only chance I'd have to escape.

I lifted my head up. My brains didn't spill out, but the pain made my eyes blur again, almost into unconsciousness. Using my feet and my elbows, I slid across the floor and propped myself up against the couch, roughly in the same spot Arlo had been in before. I know that because I was sitting on the glob of blood he'd coughed up.

Supposedly, if my TV education in private detecting was to be believed, all I had to do was rub my neck a few times and I'd be revived enough to ambush Little Billy and Arlo when they came through the door. The problem was, I couldn't lift my arm and didn't have the strength to do any rubbing.

So I resigned myself to the reality of the situation. I rested my head against the couch cushion, in case I'd jarred a chunk of my skull loose, and waited for the Pelz brothers to come back and finish what they'd started.

If, by some miracle, I survived, I was going to write a very nasty letter to the executives at TVLand about the inaccuracies in their detective programming. I was glad I'd learned this lesson from a concussion rather than a gunshot wound in the shoulder, not that it was going to make much of a difference now.

A moment or two later, I heard footsteps on the porch and turned my head to face my executioners. Only one man came in, and it wasn't who I expected.

Cyril Parkus was wearing one of those Body Glove wet suits that surfers use, and was carrying a pair of flippers and goggles. His hair was soaked and beads of water were dripping from his suit.

He'd been swimming.

"Still with us, Harvey?" he said as he padded past me in his bare, sandy feet and dropped his stuff on the table.

"Where's Arlo?" I asked, my voice raspy and weak.

"At the bottom of the lake." Cyril replied and walked into the bedroom.

I knew now that it was Cyril who'd been hiding under the porch, and that I'd made things a lot easier for him by pummeling Arlo and taping him up the way I had. The fact that Cyril was wearing a wet suit meant he'd come here planning to do exactly what he did.

When Cyril came out of the bedroom again, he was toweling his hair dry with one hand, and holding the big, serrated knife with the other.

I said, "In the morning, I suppose they'll find a boat floating in the middle of the lake without an anchor."

Cyril sat down in the chair I'd pulled out earlier and looked at me, much the same way I'd looked at Arlo.

"Can you blame me?" he asked.

I don't think he cared about my opinion, and I didn't offer it.

I thought of Arlo, his mouth taped shut, his arms and legs pinned behind him, knowing exactly what was going to happen to him as Cyril rowed the boat out into the middle of the lake. And then Cyril stopped, tied the anchor rope tightly around Arlo's ankles, and pushed him into the water. I could see Arlo wriggling helplessly as the anchor pulled him down into the murky, cold depths.

I shivered for him and for myself.

I suppose you could say Arlo deserved what he got for what he did to Jolene, but I was pretty sure Cyril didn't know about that and if he had, it wouldn't have mattered. There was only one thing that did, and that's what I asked him about.

"When did you find out that Lauren was your sister?"

Cyril stared at me. I wondered if he was going to answer me, or gut me with the Rambo knife. I think he was wondering the same thing.

"I felt it almost immediately. Every time I looked at Lauren, I saw Kelly. She was in her voice, her laugh, her eyes. It haunted me," Cyril said softly, wiping the knife blade with his towel. "I tried to tell myself I was seeing things that weren't there, but the more time I spent with her, the more certain I became. If Lauren wasn't Kelly, then she carried her spirit. I knew I was deluding myself, but I didn't care. Lauren loved me, and I loved her; it didn't matter if I imagined she was Kelly or not. Then one night after we made love, she just looked in my eyes and whispered, 'Yes, it's me.' She told me everything. And when she was done, I asked her to marry me."

I could barely lift my head, what with the pounding pain, the double vision, and waves of nausea, but I did. I stared at him, trying to bring the blur into focus.

The guy finds out that the sister he thought was dead is alive, and that he's been fucking her for weeks, and what's his first reaction?

He asks her to marry him!

It didn't make sense to me.

I mean, I could think of a lot of reactions to news like that, but a marriage proposal wasn't one of them.

"I wish I could say we lived happily ever after, but she was tormented by guilt," Cyril said. "I told her if there was a price to pay, she'd paid it long ago. She'd earned her happiness. She didn't believe it, so she threw herself into charity work, thinking that would make the guilt go away. It almost did."

How could he not understand her guilt? Didn't he think

there was anything wrong, anything unusual, about marrying his own sister?

Apparently, he didn't feel the least bit uncomfortable with the arrangement.

The only thing I could figure was that the shock of finding out who she was must have turned his brain to Cheez Whiz.

What other explanation could there be for his bizarre reaction?

And then I realized there was another one, and that it explained everything.

My vision was still a blur, but for the first time since I got involved in this case, I saw everything clearly.

"You were sleeping with your sister before," I said. "Here, at the lake, when you were teenagers."

Cyril nodded without a trace of shame. "Arlo saw us in the woods. He was going to tell, unless Kelly slept with him, too. That's why she killed herself. Only she didn't, did she? Not then, anyway."

The rest of the story I already knew or could guess. After staging her suicide, she somehow made her way to Seattle and started another life. After the car accident gave her a new face, there was nothing stopping her anymore from searching out her brother and reuniting with him as lovers once more. No one would ever know the truth about who she was.

But once again, Arlo Pelz discovered her secret.

That's what I meant about fate being cruel and inescapable. Twice Kelly Parkus had killed herself to protect her brother, only this time, she wouldn't be coming back.

I almost felt sorry for Cyril.

Then I remembered what he did to Arlo and what was probably in store for me, and he lost my sympathy.

That's when I should probably have instigated my cunning escape plan, only I didn't have one. But at that point, I couldn't even stand up on my own, much less wrestle the Rambo knife away from Cyril. There was nothing stopping him from dragging me to a boat and tossing me overboard the same way he did with Arlo.

"I guess you underestimated me, huh?" I said.

He looked up at me as if he'd forgotten I was there. "What do you mean?"

"I wasn't just the jerk in the guard shack, the clown with the iron-on badge, was I? You paid me to do a job and I did it, and then some. You sure as hell didn't expect that, not from a guy you thought couldn't pick his nose without illustrated instructions. But I found Arlo Pelz and I figured out who your wife really was, didn't I?"

I was reciting my own epitaph and I knew it.

I wanted him to know how wrong he'd been about me, how smart and capable I'd been. I wanted him to acknowledge it, if only with a nod of his head.

"You're right, Harvey, I made a big mistake hiring you." Cyril said. "I was afraid a professional detective might find out who Lauren really was. I never thought you would. Then again, a real detective would have stopped working when I fired him and wouldn't be sitting here right now."

"So what happens now, Cyril? Are they going to find two boats tomorrow morning drifting without anchors?"

Cyril rose to his feet, clutching the knife and the towel, and looked down at me. "I'm not a murderer, Harvey."

"Let's ask Arlo about that."

"That was justice. He killed my sister and I made him pay for it," Cyril said. "I've got no reason to hurt you."

"Except to stop me from going to the police and telling them what you've done."

It was only after I said it that I realized how stupid I was to say anything.

What the hell was I thinking?

Did I want him to kill me?

"I haven't done anything," Cyril said. "At least nothing that can be proved. The only person you'd be causing trouble for is yourself."

"I didn't push Arlo out of a boat with an anchor tied to his feet."

I don't know what was making me say those things, except maybe some deep-rooted death wish I didn't realize I had. Was I trying to talk him out of sparing my life?

No, I was only saying what Mannix, or Spenser, or even Rockford would in the same situation. They never let the bad guy get away with anything, even if their own lives were at stake. The bad guy had to know that the detective knew what was really going on. Now, more than ever, I felt the need to fulfill the duties of my role.

"Think a moment, Harvey. No one knows I'm here, no one has seen me. And I'll let you in on a secret: there are no plane tickets, rental car agreements, or gas station receipts proving I was here. I drove up here in my own car, paid cash for gas, and didn't stop until I got to these woods, where I waited and watched, never encountering a soul," Cyril said. "You, on the other hand, have left big tracks."

I didn't see what he was getting at; then again, I'd just suffered a concussion. I could be forgiven for being a little slow on the uptake.

"I haven't done anything illegal," I lied.

"That's not how it will look, if you are stupid enough to bring the police into this," Cyril said. "You flew up to Seattle and, masquerading as a detective, interrogated Mona Harper. You rented a car and drove to Deerlick, where you made a spectacle of yourself, going all over town asking questions about Arlo."

"So what?" I said. "I didn't kill him."

"Really? Let's look at the evidence. You beat up Arlo—his blood is all over your clothes and this cabin. You bound and gagged Arlo—your fingerprints are on the duct tape. As far as the motive, well, I'll tell them how I hired you to follow my wife and you became obsessed with her. They won't have to take my word for that; it's clear from those pictures you took of her and kept for yourself, the ones in your pocket right now. You obviously blamed Arlo for her suicide and tracked him down. To anyone objectively looking at the evidence, you killed Arlo Pelz."

His scenario was pretty damning, I had to give him that. And he didn't even know about the Sno-Inn fire, or about Jolene's murder and how I'd altered the crime scene, or about the highway robber I beat up the same way I did Arlo. If all those events were uncovered, and were looked at in the wrong way, they would only support Cyril's take on things. Even if I revealed that Lauren was Cyril's sister, it wouldn't change things for me. He'd be embarrassed and humiliated, but he wouldn't be on death row. I would be.

Yeah, he had it all worked out. I should have been happy about it, too, because it meant he didn't have to kill me. But I wasn't happy. I felt thoroughly screwed. I wasn't going to bring anyone to justice, unless I wanted to turn myself in, and I was too selfish to do that.

"That's all hypothetical, though," Cyril said. "Because no one besides us knows what happened to Arlo Pelz and nobody cares. No one is ever going to be looking for him anyway."

Except maybe the Snohomish police, to question him about Jolene's murder. They'd assume his disappearance was a flight from justice. They'd never suspect he was at the bottom of Big Rock Lake, being nibbled by fishes. And, after a while, they'd just stop looking.

Cyril wiped his prints off the knife with the towel, then tossed the weapon on the table. He gathered up his flippers and goggles and started towards the door. He must have thought we were finished. We weren't.

"That's all fine and dandy, Cyril, but don't walk out that door thinking you've fooled me or yourself," I said. "You'd have killed me if you thought you could get away with it. The only reason I'm still alive is the same reason Arlo is dead. You can't risk the truth about you and your sister coming out."

He turned around slowly.

I pulled myself up into a standing position, using all the willpower I had not to fall. I staggered, and I swayed, and had to brace myself against the couch, but at least I was facing him. I didn't want him looking down on me one second longer.

"You didn't kill Arlo for justice, you killed him to save yourself," I said. "If I turned Arlo over to the police, there would have been a trial and the truth about Lauren would have come out. You couldn't allow that. The only thing stopping you from killing me are those big tracks I left. You can't risk what an investigation into my disappearance would reveal about you and Lauren. In the end, that's all that matters to you."

Cyril shook his head sadly. "You really don't understand, do you? I don't care if anyone finds out about Kelly and me. I don't care about anything now that she's gone."

He turned and walked out.

Chapter Twenty-Four

$$\diamond \quad \diamond \quad \diamond$$

I was getting pretty good at cleaning up crime scenes.

I changed out of my bloody clothes and, once I felt clear-headed enough to drive, I went up the highway to the next town and stopped at a Seven-11. I bought some cleaning supplies and a baseball cap to hide the ugly lump on my head.

I got back to my cabin around dawn and wiped up the blood and anyplace I thought Arlo might have left his prints. At the same time, I was also unwillingly removing any trace of Cyril, too. That made me an accomplice-after-the-fact to two murders.

I wasn't proud of it.

There wasn't anything I could do about the slashed blanket on my bed. I figured if I took it, that would call more attention than the tear would. Besides, I had to believe those ratty blankets tore pretty easily, so I turned the tear into a rip and left it.

I put all the dirty paper towels, my bloody clothes, the stabbed pillow, the roll of duct tape, and the Rambo knife into a trash bag and put it the trunk of my rental car, alongside the sledgehammer and the spare tire.

I gave the cabin another quick once-over. Any other trace evidence I left behind I figured would be vacuumed up and washed away by the maid when she cleaned up the cabin for the next guest.

I was about to go, when I remembered one more thing. I went back into the bedroom, took the kitchen chair out of the closet, and returned it to its place at the table.

When I walked up to the store, Tom Wade was standing on the porch, looking out at the lake through a pair of binoculars. Betty Lou was wiping the counter with a rag and didn't see me.

"Is that one of our rowboats out there?" Wade asked.

"I don't know, Tom," his wife replied. "Why don't you go down to the beach and see if any of our boats is missing."

"I think I'll do that." He lowered his binoculars, turned around, and smiled when he saw me. "Well, good morning, Harvey. How about some breakfast?"

"I'm making pancakes," Betty Lou said.

"It will have to be next time," I said, setting my key on the counter. "I'm afraid I have an early plane to catch in Spokane."

"Let me get you a slice of pie for the road," Betty Lou said, hobbling off into the kitchen. "It will only take a minute . . ."

"Did you enjoy your stay?" Wade asked me.

"I'll never forget it," I replied.

Before I left, I borrowed Wade's binoculars, stood on the porch, and took a look at the lake. I stared at the little boat floating out on the water and wondered about all those missing anchors.

I wondered if Esme Parkus was really down at the bottom, or if she'd staged her suicide too, so she could try a new life somewhere else. And if she had, I wondered if I could find her and what I'd learn about fate if I did.

★ ★ ★ ★ ★

I dumped the contents of the trash bag in dumpsters around Spokane and tossed the Rambo knife, my BB gun, and the sledgehammer I never used into the river.

I kept the yearbook, though.

I dropped the Crown Victoria off at the EconoCar outlet at the Spokane airport; then I called Carol and told her I'd be home that afternoon.

She had a lot of questions, and I promised I'd answer them all when I got home. I was still trying to decide if I really would. I wasn't sure which would make her fall out of love with me faster, the truth about what I'd done to solve the mystery or the lies I'd have to tell to convince her I'd failed.

While I was waiting for my flight, I went to the gift shop and browsed through the selection of paperbacks for something to read on the plane. They had a lot of mysteries there, but none of them interested me. I'd lost my taste for detective stories.

Instead, I spent the three-hour flight to LA flipping back and forth through the yearbook, looking into the eyes of two young women, searching for clues to what happened to them and what might become of me.

I ransomed my car from airport parking and drove home. After driving those big cars up in Washington, my Kia Sephia felt unbearably small and cramped. But I'm not sure the tiny car was entirely to blame for my sudden claustrophobia. I was boxed-in by the stop-and-go, rush hour traffic on the San Diego Freeway and by the inevitability of the questions Carol was going to ask.

Even my own skin felt too tight. Between my cracked head and cracked ribs, it hurt to think and it hurt to breathe.

I tried to do as little of both as I could.

I could have flown halfway back to Seattle in the time it took me to drive from the airport to the Caribbean, but once I got there, I wished the journey had taken a little longer.

Carol's Toyota Camry was parked in her spot a few spaces down from mine. She'd come home early.

Stalling, I stopped at the mailbox inside the lobby and got my mail. There were a couple bills and a letter from my insurance company. It looked like a check. That was good news.

I stepped into the courtyard and the cloud of chlorine gas emanating from the pool. It was the sweet, toxic smell of home. It felt like I'd been away for years instead of days.

I went up the stairs to my apartment. I opened the door, tossed my gym bag and my mail on the couch, and stood there for a minute, just breathing the stale air and looking at the place. I used to be able to look at the beaten-up couch and the sagging bookcases and think the place felt lived-in. But I didn't see much of a life there anymore.

I closed the door and walked down to Carol's apartment. She must have heard me coming, because her door was open and she was standing there, waiting for me.

And suddenly, I realized I couldn't remember the last time anyone had waited for me, the last time anyone wanted to share what I'd felt or experienced.

Seeing her at that moment, I never wanted a woman so much in my life. I took her in my arms and kissed her hungrily. She kissed me back with just as much appetite. She pulled me into her apartment and I kicked the door shut with my foot.

We did it with a ferocity and urgency that approached

the kind of thing you see in movies, only we didn't rip our clothes into shreds, and our lovemaking was frequently interrupted by cries of pain, mostly from me. Maybe it wouldn't have hurt so much if we'd made it to the bed instead of doing it on the floor, and if I was on top instead of her, but we weren't thinking of comfort, only of slaking our need. And when it was over, about five minutes later, we lay beside each other on the floor, breathing hard, our bodies sticky with sweat and saliva and other stuff.

We lay quietly like that for a while, then she rolled on her side to face me, rested her head on her arm, and said: "Tell me everything."

So I did, without even thinking about it. I didn't leave anything out, or dress anything up so she'd still have some respect for me.

I told her about Jolene's murder, and how I'd cleaned up the crime scene to save myself. I told her how I took pleasure in the beating of the highway robber, and how later I used what I learned on Arlo Pelz. I told her how that helped Cyril drown Arlo and why Cyril did it. And I told her how I cleaned up the cabin and threw away the evidence to save Cyril and myself.

I told her the whole story while looking up at the ceiling and feeling her gaze against the side of my head like a heat lamp. It was hard enough revealing my shortcomings while I was naked; I didn't want to see the anger, the disappointment, and the disgust on her face while I did it. When I was done, I sat up with a grunt of pain and started to gather up my clothes.

"What are you doing?" Carol asked.

"Going home," I said, peering under the coffee table for my underwear. "Isn't that what you want?"

I found a sock, but no underwear.

She sat up and touched my shoulder. "You are home."

I clutched the sock, and my shirt, to my chest. "What about the things I did?"

"You did some stupid things," she said. "I'm not happy you did them. So what? You aren't a perfect person. Neither am I."

"You've never covered up a murder or beat the shit out of somebody when they were defenseless," I said. "You've got to be an idiot, a coward, and an asshole to do that."

"Yeah, that's true. But the fact you know you fucked-up, and you recognize you can be an idiot, a coward, and an asshole, goes a long way towards making up for the things you did, at least with me," she said. "Eventually, I'm going to fuck-up, and you'll see all of my failings, and you'll have to decide whether you can live with them, too."

I turned around and looked at her. I tried to keep my eyes on her face and not her breasts, because it was an important moment in our relationship, but I couldn't.

"I was planning on lying to you," I said. "I'm not sure why I didn't."

"I think I know," she said. "And that's another reason I don't want you to go. You care about me so much that it's important to you that I know you as you really are. That kind of honesty isn't easy. It was a very brave thing you did for me."

Her words had a big impact on me, and I didn't want to let her down. I wanted to continue to earn her respect, so I made another admission.

"I'm having a hard time not looking at your breasts."

"So, look at them."

"But we're having an important conversation," I said. "Doesn't it piss you off that I can't stop looking at them?"

"I'm naked; of course you're looking at them," she said.

"I'm looking at your penis."

I immediately got up and went into the kitchen for a drink of water. I wasn't really thirsty, I just needed to hide behind the counter if we were going to continue talking. I'm funny about nudity and certain kinds of conversations. I used to hate it if my shirt happened to be off, or if I was in my underwear, when my parents scolded me about something or when I had an argument with a girlfriend. It embarrassed me. It made me feel more naked than actually being naked, if you can understand that.

Carol apparently had no such hang-ups. She sat there on the floor, showing me her breasts and her crotch as comfortably as if she were wearing clothes. I was envious of her casual indifference to her own nudity.

"You haven't said anything yet about how I fucked-up the case," I said.

"Because you didn't," she replied.

"Three people are dead and I didn't bring anyone to justice for it."

She laughed. "Who do you think you are? Batman?"

It was the second time someone had said that to me since this all started, but it was the first time it made me feel foolish. Of course, when Cyril Parkus said it to me, I wasn't naked.

"I didn't accomplish anything," I said.

"You wanted to find out why Lauren killed herself and make the guy responsible pay for it. You did both."

"And I let Cyril Parkus get away with murder."

"So what? Arlo deserved it. To me, that's justice."

"Maybe there's still a way to catch Cyril without getting myself thrown in jail with him."

"Why would you even want to try?"

"Because Cyril Parkus murdered Arlo Pelz," I said. "I

can't just let him walk."

"Why not?"

Because Travis McGee wouldn't.

Neither would Joe Mannix, Lew Archer, Kinsey Milhone, Dan Tana, or Spenser.

But that's not what I said.

"Because it's wrong," I replied.

"That's not why," she said. "Don't start lying to me now, Harvey."

At that moment, I hated her for knowing me so well. I don't know how she did, since I never really talked to her before. Maybe I said more over the years than I thought I did. Maybe I'm just transparent.

"Because a private eye is supposed to solve the crime and catch the bad guys," I said. "I only did half the job. The bad guy is still out there."

The truth was, I felt cheated. I solved the mystery but I didn't get to be a hero. The only people alive who knew what I'd done were Cyril and Carol.

I was hoping for wider acclaim than that.

I was hoping to get a friend on the force.

"The bad guy was Arlo, and he's dead," Carol said. "Cyril did a bad thing, but that doesn't make him the bad guy. He lost his wife once and his sister twice and his life is shit. I have a lot of sympathy for him."

"This just doesn't feel right to me," I said. "It feels unsettled."

"Welcome to real life," she said. "You don't get tidy resolutions. People fuck-up and do terrible things, and if we're lucky, like we are now, things sort of work out. Not everyone has to feel good about it. In fact, maybe it's better for everyone if they don't."

She was right. I was looking for the TV ending, where

the whole case is wrapped up nice and neat, the bad guys are all behind bars, and the PI gets laid.

Well, at least one thing worked out the way it was supposed to.

I came around the counter and let her see me naked again, though I think I will always be naked in front of her.

"So, where do we go from here?" I asked her.

"Wherever you want."

"You're looking at my penis."

"Uh-huh," she said. "And I think I have a pretty good idea where you'd like to go."

It was a start.

Chapter Twenty-Five

$$\diamondsuit \quad \diamondsuit \quad \diamondsuit$$

I quit my job at Westland Security the next morning. I couldn't go back to sitting in that guard shack, or any guard shack, again. I had a feeling if I did, it would always remind me of a cabin closet on Big Rock Lake.

I didn't need the job anyway. If I added up my auto insurance settlement with what I had left from the Parkus job, I had about five thousand dollars. That would hold me for a few months, especially since I didn't have to buy myself a car right away. Carol was letting me drive her Camry as long as I dropped her off at work promptly at nine a.m. and picked her up at six. I think she had an ulterior motive, since the arrangement almost guaranteed I'd be spending my nights with her.

She didn't need to come up with the car arrangement for that, but I guess she was covering her bases.

The first few days I was back, I mostly lay around my apartment or hers, recuperating from my injuries, and getting used to the idea of being with Carol. I was the wounded bird in this story, though I didn't have to scrub Carol's floor or do her laundry.

I tried not to think about all the dead people. Lauren, Jolene, Arlo, even Esme. But they haunted me anyway. In my mind, they were all floating in the murky lake, all of them giving me the look that Lauren gave me before she jumped.

I can't recall Spenser being haunted by anything except his own splendid competence.

I didn't have the competence, I knew that. Still, I accomplished something, something more than writing courtesy tickets at Bel Vista Estates, even if I couldn't point to exactly what it was. And I took some big risks to do it, too.

It pissed me off that I didn't feel the euphoria and pride I felt I deserved for solving my first case and surviving.

The only thing I felt was different.

I know that's not very specific, just saying *different*. But I knew I was not the same guy I was a couple weeks ago and that I never would be again.

So, who was I now? What was I going to do?

Those were questions I'd managed to avoid my entire life and I had a feeling that keeping Carol around, and continuing to enjoy all this sex I was getting, had a lot to do with not avoiding them now.

Although my experience as a detective wasn't as much fun as I'd dreamed it would be, and I couldn't exactly use Cyril Parkus as a reference for future work, I still thought I had a certain affinity for the job. It might even live up to my expectations next time, assuming I could snag another gig. So, I started looking into what it would take to go legit, to become a licensed private detective.

What I found out wasn't encouraging.

In the state of California, you've got to take an extensive training course, log six thousand hours of investigative experience, and pass a two-hour written exam covering laws and regulations before you get a license. By my calculations, it would be about three years before I could set up shop as a private detective.

Legally, that is.

But there wasn't any law saying I couldn't go into business as an "investigative advisor" or "professional problem solver." I knew it could be done. Travis McGee didn't have a license, he just called himself a "salvage expert" and asked for half the value of whatever he recovered. I decided that could work for me, too, though I wasn't sure how I'd figure out the salvage price for, as an example, following someone's wife. I decided my task for the month would be to re-read the books and make a detailed report of exactly how McGee computed his commissions.

So that's what I was doing on that sunny Wednesday afternoon, about a week after I got back. I was on my way out to the pool in a T-shirt and shorts with one of the McGee books when I saw him, sitting on a chaise lounge, waiting for me.

Little Billy held the baseball bat across his lap, tapping it gently on the open palm of his hand, his eyes hidden behind sunglasses that were squeezed into place between his bulbous nose and his Neanderthal brow.

I was stunned and terrified and feeling incredibly vulnerable with only a used paperback and a yellow highlighter for protection. I didn't think I could muster the same tough guy swagger that enabled me to survive our last encounter.

I suppose the sensible thing to do would have been to run back into my apartment, lock the door, and hope my call to 911 would go through before Little Billy broke inside and killed me.

But curiosity and a suicidal sense of dignity got the better of me. I surrendered to the inevitability of my violent demise, smiled, and walked right over to him.

"How did you find me?" I asked.

"Arlo said he had a deal going in LA." Little Billy shrugged. "You gave your name to the Wades. I looked it up in the LA phone book. There was only one Harvey Mapes."

He had a bright future as a private eye, certainly a lot brighter than mine seemed at that moment. Then again, it occurred to me that he hadn't mentioned Cyril Parkus or Lauren Parkus. He'd only come looking for me. Which, I deduced, meant he didn't know what Arlo's deal was in LA. That gave me a slight advantage.

I motioned to the baseball bat with a nod of my head. "You brought that all the way from Deerlick?"

"I never go anywhere without it."

I guess you could call the bat his pacifier. Perhaps he just used it to pacify others. "So, when do you intend to start hitting me with it?"

"I don't know yet."

That offered me some hope. Even so, my mouth was suddenly so dry, I could hardly swallow without gagging.

"Mind if I have a Coke while you decide?" I asked.

He shrugged.

"You want anything?" I asked.

"Dr Pepper," he replied.

I went to the machine, and as I fed coins into the slot, I was struck by the absurdity of offering refreshments to my executioner. I never had experiences like this before I became a private eye and, despite the jeopardy, I wasn't sorry. I might be later, though, after a few whacks of that bat against my skull.

I brought back the drinks, reclined on the chaise lounge next to him, and took a big sip of Diet Coke.

He downed his Dr Pepper in one long gulp.

I waited for him to smash the empty can against his forehead, or crush it in his fist, or just take a bite out of it, but he didn't. He set the empty can on the ground beside him and burped.

"I want to know what happened to Arlo," Little Billy said. "He went out to the lake to kill you and didn't come back."

"Are you here to finish the job?" I asked, hoping my voice wouldn't crack and reveal my terror.

"Depends," Little Billy replied. "Did you kill my brother?"

"No."

"Then how come you're still alive?"

"Lucky, I guess."

"Why were you looking for him?"

"I can't tell you that," I replied, though if he hit me a couple times with that bat, I probably would have changed my mind. I think he knew it, too.

"I could make you," he said confidently.

"I wish you wouldn't." I tried to say that without sounding like I was pleading.

"Do you know where I can find Arlo?"

I shook my head because I didn't think I could say no with conviction.

"The police came around a few days ago. They're looking for him, too. They say he killed Jolene. Is it true?"

I nodded. "He slammed her head into a big-screen TV and left her there to die. Lovable guy, your brother."

Little Billy was silent for a moment. I was expecting the bat to come swinging my way at any second. When he finally moved, I cringed, but he was only getting comfortable on the chaise lounge. If he noticed my cowardice, he didn't show it.

"Arlo wasn't always the fuck-up," Little Billy said. "That was supposed to be my profession. But he had the hots for this girl at the lake who then went and drowned herself. After that, he didn't give a shit about anything."

Little Billy picked up the Dr Pepper can, got up, and dropped it in the trash can, then turned around and stood over me.

He was in the perfect position to swat my head right off my shoulders.

"I'm not saying what he's done is right or wrong, that don't matter to me," Little Billy said. "He's my brother, and I'm supposed to look out for him. If someone hurt him, I'm going to have to hurt them worse."

I couldn't see his eyes behind those sunglasses, but I was pretty sure he was staring at me, trying to decide if now was the time to carry out his responsibility. After a moment, he rested the baseball bat on his shoulder like a caveman's club and walked out.

I stayed on the chaise lounge for another twenty minutes or so, thinking about my encounter with Little Billy.

It occurred to me that he'd make the perfect psychopathic sidekick for my new business venture—as long as he never found out that I'd helped murder his brother.

I started staking out the gate in front of Bel Vista Estates the same afternoon I had my visit from Little Billy. I told myself I was doing it to protect Cyril Parkus in case Little Billy came after him, but the truth is, I didn't really think he was in any danger.

I told myself I'd watch him for a week, and if nothing happened, I'd leave him alone, but that wasn't true, either.

I still felt different from everybody else, like they all had secrets and it was my job to find them out. I felt such a strong compulsion now to play detective that, if I didn't have Cyril Parkus to follow, I probably would have picked somebody at random instead.

I didn't tell Carol what I was doing, though I suppose I would have told her if she'd asked. She was smart enough not to.

I'd arrive around ten a.m. after dropping Carol off at work, and would stay until about five. Cyril wasn't going to the office anymore; I'd made a call there before I started and discovered he was "on sabbatical" indefinitely. And he hardly ever came out of his house, and when he did, it was just to go down to the grocery store or drive through one of the fast-food places.

Cyril didn't look the same to me. It's not that he let himself go or anything, it was the way he walked, like he'd suddenly gained a hundred and fifty pounds, and the vacant expression on his face, like he was sleepwalking. More than once I saw him bump into a person, or collide with the edge of a grocery cart, or stumble off a curb, and not even realize it.

He was in mourning for his lost wife, his lost sister, his lost love.

I wondered if in his grief, he ever thought about what he did to Arlo, and if it mattered to him at all.

I hadn't killed anyone yet, but I thought a lot about the beatings I gave Arlo and the highway robber. I thought about how both of them were helpless at the time, and how I enjoyed that almost as much as delivering the kicks and blows. I thought about what that said about me and if I'd been changed by it.

I also thought about Carol, and I wondered if maybe, out of all the things I'd seen and done over the last few weeks, if she was what had changed me most of all.

I'd been parked outside Bel Vista Estates for five days, and was nearly finished with my list of Travis McGee's fees, on the afternoon that Cyril Parkus drove out of the gate in Lauren's Range Rover. I liked it best when he chose that car; it was much easier to see in traffic than his sleek Jag.

I was hoping he was making another trip through Taco Bell, since my stomach was growling and I was in the mood for Mexican food, but instead he headed down towards the freeway.

I thought that maybe he'd finally decided to rejoin the world again.

Traffic was light, so I stayed about four cars behind him. I wasn't worried about losing him, I could see the top of his enormous Range Rover from a block away.

He drove down to the freeway overpass that led to Old Town Camarillo, so I figured we were making a visit to the outlet mall, probably to Ralph Lauren, judging by what I'd seen of Cyril's wardrobe. It was a good sign. If he was ready to shop, he was ready to forget.

But then I saw the cars in front of me suddenly brake, and was overcome with a horrible sense of déjà vu. I stopped the car, jumped out, and ran towards the overpass, knowing what I'd see before I saw it.

Cyril Parkus stood on the guardrail over the freeway, his head turned towards the street, waiting for me to show up.

He knew I'd be there, just like Lauren knew.

And when he saw me, he smiled and looked down at the traffic as if contemplating a jump into a tranquil pool.

I yelled his name, and it was still echoing in the air when Cyril simply stepped off the rail, his arms at his sides, his body perfectly straight.

I reached the rail in time to see the massive pile-up below, cars careening across the roadway like pinballs, smashing into one another, dragging pieces of Cyril's body across the asphalt until he was lost amidst the carnage.

He'd told me in the cabin that he was going to do this, but I was so busy living out my private eye fantasy, so busy trying to plug him into the role of the big, rich, bad ugly, I didn't hear what he said.

"I don't care about anything now that she's gone . . ."

The tragedy was complete now, sparing no one. Lauren, Cyril, and Arlo were all dead. There was no wrong that had been righted. There was no bad guy on his way to life in the big house. There was no happy client to thank me for what I'd done.

In over two hundred episodes, nothing like this had ever happened to Joe Mannix.

No one was following the rules.

I turned and walked back towards my car against the frantic tide of people rushing off the street and out of their cars to see what happened. When I was passed them, I saw one person standing on the sidewalk in front of my car, a baseball bat resting on his shoulder.

"Did Parkus kill my brother?" Little Billy asked.

I nodded. Some private eye I was. He must have been following me all week, and I never once saw him. Then again, I never thought to look.

"He tied Arlo to a boat anchor and dropped him in the middle of the lake," I said, suddenly in the mood for honesty.

Little Billy took the news emotionlessly, as if I'd just told him about the weather.

"Could you have stopped him?" he asked.

"No more than I could have stopped this," I replied.

Little Billy seemed to accept that and let me pass. I was about to get in the car, but then I looked back at him standing there, and felt the pain that he wasn't showing.

The first instant I saw him, back in Deerlick, I assigned him his clichéd role in my detective story, just as I did with everybody else. He was the mindless, violent thug. The bone-breaker. One of the bad guys. Now I saw a guy whose only fault was that he cared about his brother and I didn't.

"If you want to meet me back at my place, I'll buy you another Dr Pepper and tell you everything I know," I said.

Little Billy nodded.

We both became aware of the sirens approaching, and neither one of us wanted to be here when the police showed up. I tossed him the keys to my apartment.

"I have to stop on the way and pick up my girlfriend at work," I added. "Make yourself at home."

I got into my car and watched him go in my rearview mirror.

He walked over to a rusted-out pickup truck a couple cars behind me. He'd driven all the way down here in that junker to find out the truth.

His search had ended the way mine began.

I realized then that maybe we had more in common with each other than either of us knew. Maybe we'd get the chance to find out how much. Or maybe he'd just beat me to death with his bat. I didn't know, and I didn't particularly care. I was going with my gut.

As I drove back towards LA, I threw my Travis McGee books out the window. The guy didn't know shit about being a private eye.

About the Author

◇ ◇ ◇

Lee Goldberg is a two-time Edgar Award nominee whose many TV writing and/or producing credits include *Martial Law, Diagnosis Murder, The Cosby Mysteries, Hunter, Spenser: For Hire, Nero Wolfe, Missing,* and *Monk.* He's also the author of *My Gun Has Bullets, Beyond the Beyond, Successful Television Writing, The Walk,* and the *Diagnosis Murder* series of paperback originals.